TOO MANY SUNDOWNS

Chance Benbow thought he had found the place — and the woman — which would bring him peace and quiet and a future. But then it all blew up in his face. When he recovered from the bullet wounds, he saw his future clearly, albeit clouded by gunsmoke. He would stride through it with a gun in each hand — and if hell waited on the other side, then he would meet it head-on, taking a lot of dead men with him.

JAKE DOUGLAS

TOO MANY SUNDOWNS

Complete and Unabridged

LINFORD
Leicester

First published in Great Britain in 2009 by
Robert Hale Limited
London

First Linford Edition
published 2009
by arrangement with
Robert Hale Limited
London

British Library CIP Data

Douglas, Jake.
Too many sundowns - -
(Linford western library)
1. Western stories.
2. Large type books.
I. Title II. Series
823.9′14–dc22

ISBN 978–1–84782–924–5

Published by
F. A. Thorpe (Publishing)
Anstey, Leicestershire

Prologue

Sundown

Another damn sundown!

How many does that make . . . ? A hundred? Hundred-and-fifty . . . ?

Too damn many! allowed Chance Benbow as he unbuckled his bedroll from the bay's cantle and let it drop to the coarse sand of the creek bank. The spare horse, the dun that had belonged to Donner, the one with the white spot above the left nostril, hung its head patiently, waiting to be unsaddled and hobbled for the night on the shortgrass patch where the bay gelding was already nibbling.

It was as Benbow was untying his grubsack that he smelled the cooking.

A light breeze wafted down from the timber-clad slopes of the shadowed mountain rising above the creek,

1

bringing with it the appetising odour of broiling meat. *Red meat!*

His belly rumbled as his mouth filled with saliva. It was a couple of days since he had eaten anything more than a handful of stale hardtack.

He stared up the slopes in the now fading light, but could see no signs of a fire.

That didn't surprise him: whoever was doing the cooking would make sure he didn't inadvertently provide a beacon for someone unwelcome to home in on. But the savoury trail of that meat might do just as well as a fire full ablaze on the slope to lead him where he wanted to go.

He retied the near-empty grubsack on to the saddle horn, heaved the bedroll back on to the cantle and buckled up the straps again. *Man, he ached!* Every damn bone and joint, scalp to toenails. He flexed his fingers and heard the small cracks and creaks as each one in turn stiffened and curled into his palm.

Much more of this endless sleeping out of doors in sweat-damp clothes or dew-wet blankets that never got a chance to dry and he'd have worse rheumatics than old Happy Jackson, owner of the livery stables in Loma Vista.

It wouldn't matter! he told himself angrily. *Rheumatics, lung fever, gut-shot or backshot, he would continue . . . ! Nothing this side of Hell was going to stop him!*

He settled into the bay's saddle with a grunt, and reached back for the dun's trailing reins, making a small sound with the effort it cost him. The left arm was coming good: slowly, but getting there.

Then he touched his spurs to the bay and started riding, picking his way warily up the slope . . .

There was still an afterglow by the time he had climbed high enough to see the red, glowing coals and the steaks threaded on to an angled green stick, sizzling and sputtering in the radiating heat.

An occasional gobbet of fat fell, to flare briefly as it reached the coals. In the flash of light from one of these tiny flares, he saw the man standing beside the boulder bulking a couple of yards from the fire, with a crudely built mountain shack a dark blob behind him.

He was holding a rifle and working the lever very fast. 'Stop there!'

Benbow halted, hands folded on the saddle horn. He nodded briefly, not sure whether the man could see the movement.

'Thought you'd've had a shell in the breech, all ready, *amigo*.'

'I'm ready. Heard you comin' minutes ago.'

'Meant you to. Figured anyone who took the trouble to hide his cabin as well as this one might be a shade trigger-happy if he heard someone sneakin' around — 'specially right on sundown.'

A short silence, then, 'Who says I'm hidin'?'

4

'Not you. I said you did a mighty good job of hidin' your cabin. I couldn't even see it from below, and that was before the sun dropped behind the crest and put this slope in shadow.'

A grunt. 'Well, what you want?'

Benbow gestured, moving his left hand carefully so as not to spook the other man. 'One of those steaks if you can spare it. Smelled it down by the creek — and I see you've got a butchered deer carcass hanging back there in the trees, well out of a coyote's reach.'

'You see too damn much, friend. 'Specially in light fadin' as fast as this. Still, never thought about cookin' smells bringin' someone in. But I'll remember.'

Benbow waited patiently, his right hand resting on top of his left on the saddle horn, giving this man time to decide what his next move was going to be.

'What you doin' here?'

Benbow gestured towards the crest of

the dark bulk of the mountain. 'Headin'' up and over to Ryker's Springs.'

It was a fair enough answer; lots of riders chose to go over the mountain rather than use the longer trail around the base.

But the man assessed this rider carefully, being naturally wary and suspicious of strangers. And he wanted to have this stranger sized up properly before the light faded too far for him to be sure of what he might see or read in that stubbled face.

Even leaning forward slightly the way he was, he looked to be tall in the saddle. Rifle scabbard under his left leg. Single Colt in a holster on his thigh, the leather looking worn but well cared for. Square-jawed, the stubble thick with trail dirt, weathered clothes spattered with it. Horses well-travelled but had been looked after . . .

Whoever he was, this ranny had come a far piece.

Question was 'why?' and did it have anything to do with him . . . ?

Then he frowned, looking from the dun to Benbow sharply, as another dribble of fat flared up.

'What's that dark patch on the dun's saddle?'

'Blood.'

The man grew a quick inch with this news as he straightened a little, the rifle barrel lifting about the same distance. 'Yours?'

Benbow shook his head — just once.

'Where's the rider?'

'Dead.'

The man's hands were restless on the rifle now, opening and closing on the wood and metal as the sweat began to form. He moved his feet a little, shuffled to one side, on to flatter ground, keeping Benbow covered.

Only the rider's eyes moved, watching the other's every movement.

'You can't bring your troubles here, mister!'

'Not aimin' to. He had three pards, the owner of the dun. They're all dead, too.'

The man's rifle came up, more threatening now. The coals even caught the glint in his eyes.

'Jesus! Who the hell are you?'

'Chance Benbow. Don't you know me?'

The man shook his head emphatically. 'How could I? I've never seen you before.'

'You seen my woman.' The voice was low now, accusing.

'What're you talkin' about? I dunno your woman! I dunno *you!* Dunno what you want, where you're from, nothin'. And I don't wanna know!'

'I'm from down Socorro way, a little to the northeast. Ensuelo Valley.'

'That's a helluva long ways off!'

'You were there at least once.'

'Me? Not me, mister. I ain't never been anywhere near Socorro in years.'

'How about last fall? Think about it.'

'Last fall . . . ?' The man snorted. 'Don't have to think too hard about that! I was buildin' a road through the Santa Fe Valley — courtesy the chain gang from the local hoosegow. Still got the damn calluses on my hands.'

'Show me.'

'Wha — ? Like hell! I'd have to set down the rifle to do it and I ain't — '

'Then set it down!' The stranger's voice was suddenly hard, cold, demanding.

It scared the man with the rifle and he took a firmer grip on the weapon.

'Listen, Benbow. Sounds to me like you're after someone. Well, it ain't me! I dunno what the hell you're talkin' about!'

'Ask the others — when you meet up with 'em in hell.'

'No — wait! W-a-i-t!'

A brief, ragged crash of gunfire rolled across the darkening mountain.

The rifle got off a shot, the bullet passing with a rush of hot air past the hard planes of Benbow's face, revealed now by the powder flashes of the two shots he fired from his Colt.

The man went down, twisting, rifle

clattering as he fell back against the boulder, slid down the wind-sculpted rock and sprawled at its base.

Benbow dropped out of the saddle, went down on to one knee, Colt still smoking, hammer cocked, as he turned the man on to his back. Glazing, terrified eyes stared up at him.

'You're Troy McWilliams, ain't you?' The man nodded, gurgling as blood spilled over his lips. 'Then you're the one I wanted — along with Ryan, Silver, Donner and Harris. You're the last one.'

The wide eyes stared up, unblinking, but with a faint cloud of puzzlement. 'I ain't — rid with them — for mebbe three months — longer. We split — after Deadwood . . . '

'But you met up again near Loma Vista last fall!'

'Man — you're loco.' A bout of coughing shook the dying man and, gasping, he made ragged sounds that turned Benbow's blood cold.

McWilliams was trying to . . . laugh!

'F-funny.' The wounded man gagged on the word.

'You got a damn queer sense of humour!'

The head lolled loosely. 'I been a — bad bastard all my life. Now you — you've killed me for somethin' I din' do!' A hand clawed weakly at Benbow's shirt sleeve. 'Ain't that — funny?'

1

Backshot

One summer earlier, Chance Benbow had been straddling the top roof beam of his partly completed cabin in the Grand Quivira Mountains. He was hammering home the last few hardwood pegs of the day when he heard gunfire from down the valley. A long way down the valley.

Just a short, ragged volley, but a mix of rifles and at least one six-gun. Then silence, drawn out. No more shooting. He glanced at his rifle propped up below, waited a little longer, then returned to his chore.

Not much gunfire was ever heard in this valley, but — whatever it was, it hadn't seemed too intense. *Don't fool yourself: it was no group of hunters.* He returned to his chore.

Sundown was close but the air was still hot and oppressive. Sweat plastered his dark work-shirt to his muscled upper body and trickled down his face to drip from his strong, stubbled jawline. He was thinking of the creek, glanced towards it, almost straight into the sinking sun, as he prepared to drive home the very last peg. But he checked the final hammer blow, hitching around slightly, the tool still poised. He adjusted his curled hat-brim, cutting down some of the glare.

Something moved out there, between him and the sun. The light was turning from burning gold to crimson, like the glow of a furnace door.

Another stinking hot one tomorrow, he thought as he stretched a little more, seeking his target. *There!*

A rider, coming out of the sunset, sagging in the saddle. Benbow shifted again: it was difficult to see clearly with that blazing colour hurled into glare-weary eyes after a day's work in the scorching sun. The horse might be hurt, too, or, more likely, had been ridden hard and fast. But it would bring the rider up here in ten minutes or less.

He swung down, hanging by his hands a moment before dropping amongst the sawdust and wood-shavings and scattered off-cuts of timber. He took time as he brushed himself down to look at his progress. Not bad, for a couple of weeks' work alone. By God, his shoulders still ached from felling the lodgepole pine trees, trimming and cutting, splitting with iron wedges, cursing innumerable splinters and blunt tools. Not to mention the buzzing insects. He was making progress, though he would've liked to have got more done.

He hadn't yet found his woman. Well, maybe he had. Ivy Cartwright was desirable — and available — but old man Cartwright would demand a decent house, a cattle herd and property that could be worked up into something profitable in the future, before he would grant permission for her marriage. And he had made it known that he would believe a drifter like Chance Benbow could settle and proved up on a quarter-section only when he saw it happen — with the deeds, signed and sealed by the Government Land Agency. *Then* he would likely want to see a bank balance and — Oh, hell! He might as well forget about Ivy Cartwright . . . Easier said than done!

His wanderings down the twisted trails of his constant worries had briefly made him lose sight of the rider coming in out of the west. But he picked up the movement again as the horse splashed across the creek, the man still hunched, leaning to one side now. He came out of the deeper shadow of the run of trees and into the crimson light of the slope where the partly built cabin sat, with its fine view over the bend of the deepwater creek.

Benbow swept up his rifle from where he had propped it alongside a bowsaw and a pickaxe, quickly levered a shell into the breech as the staggering mount made its way up the last of the slope. Benbow raised his eyes to the creek and beyond.

There was no pursuit that he could see. Then he gave attention to the newcomer. He couldn't see any blood from here. The man was hatless and his face was etched in the blood-red sundown, showing pain and strain, cuts and bruises. His holster was empty. He lifted a hand slightly, gasping in a grating voice, 'Sorry to — trouble you like this . . .'

Then he toppled to the ground and the panting mount stepped awkwardly aside.

Benbow saw the blood then — on the back of the ragged shirt, just under the left shoulder.

At the same time he heard another rider plunging his mount across the creek. A medium-sized man, forking a big Arab-looking claybank — and holding a rifle in one hand.

'Get away from him!' he called

hoarsely, urging his mount up the slope.

But he slowed when Benbow lifted the rifle. 'Far enough!'

'Hell with you! I want that son of a — '

He hauled rein fast as Benbow put a bullet into the ground a foot in front of the claybank. The horse veered left and the rider was busy fighting the reins for a moment. He sat the still-nervous mount, glaring out from under a narrow-brimmed hat.

'By God, fella! You dunno what you're gettin' into!'

'Tell me.'

At the same time the rider's rifle on the side away from Benbow suddenly came up and across his body, triggering. Benbow staggered as a bullet ripped through his shirt and took him in the upper left arm. He instinctively dropped to one knee and his Winchester hammered a brief, fast volley, lever working in a blur, pain knotting his now bleeding arm.

The rider fired again but too late: two of Benbow's bullets took him in the upper body and hurled him from the saddle. He hit hard, sliding, the claybank leaping aside, eyes wide, body quivering, as it snorted warily.

Benbow stood, another cartridge in the rifle's breech now. He glanced at the stranger who had been backshot, but he hadn't moved. Then he warily approached the man he had just shot off the claybank.

He was sprawled on his back, staring sightlessly up at the burning sky, which was reflected in the scratched brass sheriff's star pinned to the bloody shirt front . . .

'He could've called out that he was a damn lawman,' complained Benbow as he doctored the wound in the back of the man who had arrived first.

He was stretched out on one of Benbow's blankets in the shadows. He was barely conscious, one eye swollen almost shut, and had done a lot of cussing while Benbow dug the bullet out from under his left shoulder blade. He murmured something now but the words were muffled against the bent arm on which his head was resting. He had a friendly face, now grimacing with his pain.

'How'd you get it in the back?'

'B-bushwhack.'

Benbow frowned, still mopping up the bleeding wound. 'I heard several shots. Posse?'

The head of sweaty, short brown hair moved slightly. 'Just Casey . . . ' He rolled his good eye towards the man with the star, 'plus Feeney and — and Dekker.'

Benbow's frown deepened. 'I've heard those last two names recently. Couple of wanted stage robbers.'

The head moved again in a minute movement that could have been a nod. 'Casey's — no — lawman. Took that badge off — a sheriff he dry-gulched near Magdalena.'

Benbow felt some relief; it had been self-defence, shooting that rider down,

19

but if he had *really* been a sheriff . . .

'That gospel?' When the man nodded wearily, Benbow said, quietly, 'What does that make you?'

'Name's Wylie — work for Wells Fargo. Been — after them — three — walked into — a beatin' and — ambush.'

It was costing him plenty to gasp out even these few words and Benbow squeezed his shoulder — noticing the congealing threads of blood on the back of his own hand, which had run down from his wound. It was throbbing now and he used his teeth to tighten the kerchief he had tied over the bullet gouge on his upper arm as he told Wylie his name.

A grunt, which probably was an acknowledgement. 'Am I — hit real bad?'

'Well, I'm glad I don't have that wound. But I figure it'll come right in time. We're a long way from a town here, though, and a sawbones. Nearest'd be Loma Vista.'

'Sorry to — interrupt your work. Looks like it'll be a good — cabin.'

'In time. Don't worry about it. I'll take you into Loma Vista tomorrow and see about some proper treatment for the wound.'

One hand groped awkwardly for him. 'No — I'll be OK. Don't feel too . . . bad. It hasn't hit my — lung.'

'Well, you're in the best position to know that. But, if blood-poisonin' sets in there's nothin' I can do. Be safer if you see a doctor.'

'Well — mebbe — but . . . You're busy. Don't want to — disrupt things. You just — do your best — for me. I'm pretty tough and I heal fast . . . I can — pay.' He saw the change come over Benbow's face out of the corner of his upper eye. 'Wrong thing to say, huh? I'm — sorry.'

'Christ, man, you're apologizing all over the place!'

'I'm sorr — Habit. I'll try to — remember — but — I — I'd rather no one knew I was — working this part of the — country.'

'Casey knew.'

'Have to find out how that happened. Later. Let me stay here a while, Benbow. You can work. I'll be all right in the . . . shade, where you can keep an . . . eye on me.'

Benbow studied him in silence; it wasn't quite a plea, but this stranger sure wanted to stay away from other folks. Benbow had had times like that.

'I know a little carpentry. When I'm feelin' better — could even lend you a hand . . . '

It was mighty tempting and Benbow wanted to agree — but that wound was ugly; not so deep, but the slug had skidded off the shoulder bone, had maybe even fractured it. There were all kinds of complications that could set in.

But at the same time . . . He glanced at the silhouetted skeleton framework of the cabin above the four levels of wall logs he had managed to lay by himself. He'd nearly broken his damn back doing it. He'd need help to raise the walls higher. By the time he was ready to do that, Wylie should be much healed and . . .

Sooner the cabin was finished, sooner he could approach Old Man Cartwright — and Ivy . . . but he wasn't easy about taking a chance with another man's life . . .

He told Wylie so and they argued. In the end, Benbow cursed himself for allowing Wylie to talk him around — like he'd wanted to happen all along! Deep down, he would rather it was this way, stay out here and get on with building the cabin . . . But if anything happened to Wylie, a Wells Fargo man . . .

'What happend to Feeney and Dekker? They with Casey when he backshot you?'

Wylie nodded.

'Where are they now?'

'Hell, I guess.' The pain-filled eyes held to his steadily. 'I'm a pretty good rifle shot. Most Wells Fargo undercover men have to be.'

'I heard a pistol, but mostly rifles.'

'Had a rifle — picked off Feeney and Dekker. Then it jammed. Had to use my six-gun. Thought I'd finished Casey.'

Well, Benbow knew Wells Fargo wouldn't send a man into the field if he was an amateur: if Wylie was what he claimed, of course . . .

He had a hunch the man was telling the truth, though; but he would keep a very close eye on him just the same.

And on that trail coming into the valley out of the west and across the creek.

2

Loma Vista

Wylie was right about one thing: he was a fast healer.

But while the bullet wound itself healed over, it had obviously sapped a good deal of his strength. The beating he had taken hadn't helped much although the bruising was fading to a greenish yellow now instead of purple. He stumbled about, trying to help, stacking timber close to where Benbow was working, but he needed plenty of rest stops and he drank gallons of coffee. Or it seemed that way to Benbow. His stores had been meagre to start with; he tried to stretch them as far as possible, supplementing where he could with a day's hunting meat when he would grudgingly take time off from cabin-building.

'I'm a good shot,' Wylie said. 'I can get us meat.'

Wiping sweat from his eyes, Benbow looked at the man. His face was haggard and drawn with pain, if not strain from trying to do more than he ought. He had lost weight and twice Benbow had had a scare when he was sure fever was setting in. That would have meant infection and then there would have been no choice but to get Wylie to a doctor.

'You'd kill yourself, trying to track and shoot a deer up on that mountain.'

'Don't have to be deer, does it? Jackrabbits make a fine stew.'

'And run like the wind. You'd need to spend all day looking for their burrows and lofts. Thanks, anyway, Wylie, but I'm getting short of nails and I've chipped the blade of my big plane. There're other things I can pick up, too.' (All at Cartwright's store where Ivy served behind the counter.) 'So I'll take time for a run into town.' He looked steadily at Wylie. 'You could come and have the doc look at you. To be on the safe side.'

Wylie was quick to shake his head. 'No. Wound's healing fine. Really. Ribs still creak some and I know I need building up but I'm feeling a little stronger each day. I can finish some of the flooring in the bedroom if you lay the planks across the beams. Use up the rest of the nails — and I can repair that short ladder with the busted rungs. How long will you be?'

'Couple of days. You want me to send a wire to Wells Fargo?'

Wylie went very still, then found some gunk on his boot lace and bent to pick it off with his thumbnail. 'Why?'

'Let 'em know you're OK.'

'No need. I'm my own boss on assignment. They don't expect me to check in unless I've got something to report.'

'Well, you have, haven't you? You've caught up with Casey.'

For the first time since his arrival, Wylie showed a hard face, more annoyance than anger. Most times he was over-eager, trying to please — almost *desperate* to please.

'Look, Chance, don't worry about me. I've been doin' this job for years. I know when and when not to contact head office.'

Benbow nodded slowly. 'Sure. How about a new shirt? That old one I gave you won't last much longer.'

Wylie suddenly grinned. 'Yeah, could do with another shirt. Yours are all too big anyway. I don't have much cash.'

Benbow waved it aside and began to prepare for the run into Loma Vista. He would take the buckboard, and tie his mount to the tailgate.

There was no permananet law in Loma Vista; the Socorro sheriff visited or sent up a deputy occasionally or on request. So he wouldn't have the bother of reporting the deaths of Casey and his friends.

He had buried Casey in a small cave, before collapsing the entrance. One day it had rained and Wylie, for once, took to his bed in the shelter of the overhanging rock where Benbow had set up camp. Chance took the time to ride up-valley and eventually found the place where Wylie had been ambushed by Casey, Feeney and Dekker. Tracks were practically unreadable but he found the two dead men. The wild animals had left enough for him to see that each had two or three bullet wounds — from rifle bullets, so that backed up Wylie's story about his rifle jamming before using his six-gun on Casey. He found a cutbank and dragged the bodies there, caving in the earth and rock over the remains. The men's horses were still in the vicinity, still saddled. He easily caught the animals and removed the saddles.

Both horses had a little skin rubbed off but had not yet developed sores, so he took them back to the cabin site and turned them into the corral with his own four horses and Casey's. Wylie's mount had been badly wounded so he had led it out into a dry gulch and put it out of its misery.

Wylie had looked at him, tight-lipped, on his return from the valley. 'My story check out?'

It was a curt query, and Benbow thought there was a flash of belligerence in the glare-reddened eyes.

'Sure. I cleaned things up a little.'

After getting the details, Wylie's face softened and he nodded. 'Sorry to put you to all that trouble — '

'Forget it,' Benbow snapped: he was growing a little tired of Wylie's frequent 'sorrys'.

When he was ready to leave for town he hesitated, noting again Wylie's obvious weakness.

'You rest up. Forget the cabin. I've left all the grub so you don't need to do anything but build up your strength. See you in a couple of days.'

'Bring me some tobacco, will you? Don't want to use all of yours.'

Was that yet another way of damn well apologizing?

'Yeah, sure. *Adios*.'

'Er — I'd feel better if I had a gun.'

'Casey's Colt and rifle are amongst that pile of gear somewhere. His bullet belt, too.'

Wylie nodded, smiling now. *Relief?*

Benbow flicked the reins and the buckboard started towards the creek ford a little way upstream. He paused when he reached it, looked back. Wylie was still standing in the shade of the one high wall of the cabin that they had raised so far: the effort had made Wylie move like a man of seventy for a couple days afterwards and the wound even oozed a little blood. But it did not burst open as Benbow had been afraid might happen.

He sure don't want anyone to know where he is, Benbow thought as the buckboard rumbled and clattered across the ford. *He sure as hell don't.*

★ ★ ★

Ivy Cartwright smiled as she placed the sack of coffee beans in the box with the rest of Benbow's order. She had reddish-brown hair, and lots of it, surrounding a face that was neither long nor round: 'pleasant' was how Benbow thought of it, with its small nose, wide mouth and green eyes. He had seen those eyes touched with mischief and, once or twice, narrowed in anger. Not that she was bad-tempered, but Ivy was strong-willed when she wanted to be. Mostly she was . . . accommodating, he figured as the best word. *And lovely — warm.*

She liked people and was genuinely interested in their talk, whether it be some old spinster's complaints about noisy neighbour children or the expectations and fears of a young ranch wife nearing birthing time of her first child. She had a sympathetic and usually practical response, sending most folk away with a smile, or at least feeling better about their problems.

And Ivy Cartwright had a good-sized problem of her own, in the shape of her father, Big Dave. He owned a large cattle spread down the eastern side of the vast valley — the D-C, the latter letter hooked through the bottom of the first for the brand. It was by far the biggest ranch in the county.

As well, he owned the general store — the only 'big' store in town — and had an interest in a company back East that was considering bringing a railroad spur to Loma Vista in the not-too-distant future. He was probably the richest and most powerful man in the county, if not that part of the Territory.

And he had only one child: Ivy. So any man who came with notions of a-courting needed not only a solid background in the cattle industry but a fair share of sheer guts even to think about such a thing.

Chance Benbow had given it a lot of thought before he had made his intentions clear; not that Cartwright scared him in any way: power backed by riches never had bothered him, but he wondered whether he could make a good showing as a small rancher, with a tolerable chance to become a 'big' rancher sometime in the future, and provide for a wife and future family.

In Ivy's upbringing she had wanted for nothing, but she hadn't been spoiled. Her mother, who had died in a riding accident five years ago, had made sure that she attended all the right schools and, as part of her education, had given Ivy the correct outlook on life. She would have been proud of her daughter had she lived long enough to see the results.

Dave Cartwright took over Ivy's life then — she allowed him to think he did, anyway — and he had scared off half the eligible and not-so-eligible young men in the south-west.

But not Chance Benbow; he was obstinate, stubborn, kept showing up, whether invited or not. And Ivy had obviously approved, so Dave had enquiries made, expensive enquiries, and wasn't too impressed with what he learned.

Benbow came from a family in

Virginia with tobacco interests — and *that* was a plus, right off. But he had left home early to go see this huge land, deliberately cutting all ties with the family — not on bad terms (at least not on his part, although an elder sister and brother were hostile). Chance simply wanted to be independent. He wasn't afraid to get his hands dirty and he was quick to learn. A good rider right from the start, he tried his hand at trapping and breaking-in mustangs, working with a bunch of tough professionals. He set his own standards and had killed a man for ill-treating a horse that was stubborn to come to the bridle and bit. It was a legitimate shoot-out, with the other man reaching for his gun first. Benbow had been wounded but, down in the dust, he had still shot and killed the other.

After recovering he went out and found a man with a rising reputation as a gunfighter. He learned a few tricks; he had the discipline to practice to the point of tedium — and then practice some more until his mentor considered he was proficient. The day that point was reluctantly reached by the master, the gunfighter lost his final conflict in the middle of a muddy street in Deadwood, falling to the challenger's gun not six feet from where Benbow stood.

The winner, flushed and excited, brashly threw down the gauntlet to Benbow on the spot.

'You've wasted your time, fella. Whatever he taught you ain't enough! Drag your iron if you think me wrong.'

Benbow had done just that, said '*I do*,' and had paid for the funeral of the challenger along with that of the man who had taught him.

That kind of impressed Dave Cartwright: 'A man with more than just a conscience — a strong sense of fair play. Perhaps, even . . . integrity.'

He read eagerly through his investigator's reports, searching for news of Benbow's subsequent gunfights as he drifted through the country, working the cattle trails, trying his hand at prospecting — and having only his second gunfight, with claim-jumpers, accounting for two and wounding a third who was later lynched as a thief by the other seekers on the goldfield.

Cartwright was somehow disappointed that he could learn of only three more gunfights over the next couple of years before Benbow, broke and refusing to call upon his family who were certainly rich enough to support him, joined the cavalry for a short stint. Dave had learned little about that time, except that Benbow had quit, sickened by the Indian Wars and their bloody punitive raids.

He hired out in a couple of range wars but there had been no outstanding gunfights or overly violent incidents.

He was shaping up into quite a human being and Cartwright grew restless; deep down he didn't want Benbow to come out smelling of roses. He wanted to find something he could get his teeth into, a legitimate reason to refuse him marriage to Ivy.

He didn't see himself as being selfish, only as wanting the best for his only daughter.

Ivy knew the truth, though, and while she was only twenty, a few months short of her majority, when she would be able to make up her own mind, she kept silent, waited patiently to see just how far her father would go.

Convinced at last that nothing short of murder would prevent Benbow from courting Ivy — he had considered having Chance beaten by some of his hardcases, but had discarded the notion — he had then come up with his conditions:

'Prove up on that miserable quarter-section out there in the Quiviras, well within the time limit, and with every requirement fulfilled — I'll have no shortcuts or bribing officials to ignore work not properly done, and you'll have a herd of good beeves. I'll sell you some, but I tell you now you'll pay top market price: no concessions.'

'I'll find my own herd,' Benbow told him, seeing the man start back in his chair a little. 'I'll work the hills and bring in mavericks to swell the numbers.'

'By God! Most of those mavericks in the hills are probably mine anyway!'

'If there're no brands on 'em, they're fair game, you know that. Law of the range.'

Cartwright looked ready to spit fire and brimstone. 'You cocky son of a bitch!'

'How'd you first start your herds, Mr Cartwright?'

Dave chewed on his lower lip. 'Never you mind about me. You're the one has to prove up! And you'll need a decent bank balance and — '

Benbow stood abruptly, making the rancher blink. 'Let's cut it short: you want to make things as hard as possible for me. OK. Make your list. I'll work through it and by the time I've finished — why it might even be in time for Ivy's twenty-first birthday — and your

39

damn conditions'll no longer matter.'

Dave Cartwright wasn't used to such talk and he fairly steamed for a moment, then said, confidently, 'What makes you think Ivy won't want — and demand — all the things on my list?'

'She may. But my bet is she's ready to wait, see them accumulate gradually as we build up the spread.'

'Don't put too much hope in that 'we', mister!'

Benbow was willing to let him have the last word. He nodded curtly and left.

But things went slowly for Benbow: he found that getting supplies wasn't easy; there were always 'delays', 'shortages', 'shipping foul-ups', unless Ivy managed secretly to cut a few corners and work around the obstacles Cartwright was deliberately putting in Benbow's way.

'You don't play fair, Dad,' she told Dave. 'This isn't one of your business deals, no holds barred, where you can use our supply lines to make things difficult for your competitors — this is *me*! My future.' She took a deep breath and added with a rush, 'You will not endear yourself to me if you prevent Chance Benbow from proving up.'

Cartwright stared at the door of the ranch office as it closed hard enough behind her to shake in its frame.

By God! She'd never spoken like that to him before! Maybe — maybe he ought to take another look at what plans he had been forming to teach this cocky Virginian a lesson . . .

'And damned if I like being pushed into doing that!' he said aloud.

But, while there was tension between Ivy and her father, she knew that no matter what happened, she could not marry before her twenty-first birthday without Big Dave's permission. *He knew it, too.*

'Stubborn old man!' she told herself, forgetting she had inherited a good deal of that same stubbornness. 'Still — I love him just the same . . .'

He hadn't always been good to her

mother and it was only after her death that Big Dave admitted this to himself.

Conscience-stricken, frustrated because he could never set the matter right now, he determined that no man was going to treat his daughter so off-handedly. He didn't realize that, by the standards he was setting, there would be no man in the entire United States good enough to become Ivy's husband. Or maybe he did realize it.

Ivy knew this and so did Chance, but he refrained from pointing it out to her. And she blessed him for his forbearance; no matter what Dave thought or said or did, she knew Chance Benbow was the man for her.

★ ★ ★

'You've doubled up on your supplies this time, Chance,' she said now as he took money from his pocket to pay his bill.

'Extra mouth to feed.' At her puzzlement and after counting out the correct money, he told her about Wylie.

'Is he . . . what he says he is?'

He could detect the worry in her voice. 'I think so. It's kinda strange not wanting to let Wells Fargo know he's OK and that the stage-robbers have been taken care of, but he is an undercover man, so I guess there could be some reason for it.'

'But — if he is lying . . . ?'

'Then he's using my place as a hideout. It'll show sooner or later.'

'He seems . . . dangerous.'

'Could be. But I'll read the signs and be ready. I reckon he's OK. Quiet sort, always afraid of puttin' people out, apologizing. I get fed up with it, but he seems to feel he's gotta do it.'

'Well, you take darn good care, Chance!' She smiled as she spoke, closed one small hand over his big, tanned callused one. 'I don't want to be a widow even before the wedding.'

He grinned. 'You'll have to work that one out for me. Don't make sense.'

Her smiled faded. 'Don't make fun!

You know what I mean!'

He sobered. 'Sure. I'm stayin' over tonight. Want to have supper with me somewhere?'

'What about right here?'

'Is . . . Dave in town?'

'No! He's out at the ranch. We'll have the living quarters to ourselves.'

'I knew there was somethin' that'd make this long ride worthwhile.'

3

Trial by Violence

Benbow made arrangements to sleep in the livery, Tad Byron taking the dollar and saying, a mite slyly, 'Dunno as how I'd have the will power to prefer sleepin' on a pile of straw in the loft to a nice warm bed — in the same house as a fine-lookin' woman like . . . '

He stopped short of mentioning Ivy's name when he saw Benbow's face. Byron licked his lips. 'Aw, I was just joshin', Chance.'

'Only reason you're still standin', Tad.'

Byron blew out his cheeks as Benbow left the livery. The man had washed up and slicked his hair with water at the washbench outside, brushed down his clothes. He looked presentable enough as he returned to the rear door of the general store, now closed for the night. Jimmy Tuttle, the yard man, was just locking up the storeroom and nodded to Benbow as he went into the living-quarters of the store.

Ivy had made a savoury stew, reheated from what was left over from the night before, actually, and while they ate it she had an apple pie baking in the big wood-range oven.

It was the best meal he had had in weeks and he said so. The living-quarters behind the store were roomy: kitchen, small parlour, two bedrooms upstairs, and a small office for doing the accounts, plus a medium-sized storeroom attached to one end.

'We'll have our coffee and pie in the parlour,' Ivy said and he went on ahead, sprawled on the sofa and rolled a cigarette while he waited. He had just lit up and was exhaling smoke when she arrived. She set down the tray holding the coffee pot with cups, sugar and cream bowls and two slices of golden-crust apple pie. Then she took the cigarette from his fingers and sucked in a small drag. She coughed a little. 'I don't know what you see in tobacco!'

'Well, it ain't the same as what my family sees.' He spoke lightly but she sensed that sometimes he wished he was closer to his family up there in Virginia — in both distance and affection. He rarely mentioned them and she had often wondered if there had been some — incident — to cause him to leave in the first place. Getting right down to it, she didn't know a lot about Chance Benbow, but what she did know, she approved of.

'Coffee's too hot. And the pie needs to cool a little.'

She worked around almost on to his lap and began toying with some ragged strands of his still-wet hair. 'I can give you a haircut before you leave.'

'It'll do.'

She tapped his stubbled cheek lightly with two fingers. 'Sometimes you are bone-headed, Chance Benbow. Oh, don't look like that! *You are*! I'm just thinking of some reason to delay your departure.'

'Better watch your reputation. I'll bet there's half a dozen folk already hopin' to run into Dave so they can tell him I spent a couple hours with you here.'

'Let them! Dad knows I wouldn't do anything wrong.'

'He might give *you* the benefit of the doubt — '

'Oh, you tread *too* carefully where he's concerned! D'you think *he* wasn't young and in love once?'

'Can he remember?'

'Oh! Come here and kiss me! It's been weeks and I'm starved to feel your arms about me. I feel so — safe at such times and . . . '

Of course, in the middle of the long, hungry kiss, Dave Cartwright came crashing in, eyes bulging, clothes trail-stained and dusty, a quirt swinging in his big left hand.

'By Godfrey! Jimmy Tuttle was right! You are sneakin' in here behind my back!'

'Dad! Don't!'

Cartwright strode in swinging the quirt. Benbow set Ivy rather roughly aside so that she overbalanced and slipped off the edge of the sofa with a small cry. He came to his feet, left arm rising to parry the quirt. He grabbed Cartwright's thick wrist and twisted, but Big Dave resisted, teeth bared, breath hissing through flared nostrils with his efforts.

Benbow had his work cut out but he eventually twisted the quirt free, tossed it across the room and thrust the big rancher away. Dave staggered, started forward again but Ivy clung to his arm, stopping him.

'*Dad*! For heaven's sake! You've got it all wrong! Chance and I have just had supper and — '

'Now he's lookin' for dessert!'

'You got a dirty mind, Dave,' Benbow said tightly. 'It's your daughter you're insulting, not me!'

'It's *you*! You're the culprit, workin' your damn charms on a girl not even old enough to know her own mind!'

'Stop it!' Ivy snapped, stamping her foot, making Dave Cartwright pause, blinking. 'Dad, you know me better. Chance and I weren't doing anything wrong, nor intending to. He's just in town overnight. *Let me finish!* He's just in town overnight and then he's going back to continue building his — our ranch.'

Cartwright frowned. 'Is — is that how you think of it now? Yours — and his?'

'Of course I do! After we're married, it's where we'll be living and — '

'You're running on ahead, girl! You're a long ways from marryin' this trail scum! Believe me, you are!'

He stormed out and Ivy couldn't hold back the tears any longer. Benbow hesitated a little and then folded her in his arms. She cried softly and the way he felt the rackings of her slim body, he knew she had been holding in too much for too long. He eased her down on to the sofa.

'Ivy, I'm sorry this has happened.' *Hell, he sounded just like Wylie!* 'But I'd best go now. Dave'll calm down. Looks like he's been driving some cows in and has had a rough trail.'

'I should have remembered. He was to deliver two of his seed bulls to Asa McGill. Probably came in with a couple of the ranch hands. He'll put up at the saloon and I'll see him in the morning.' She stood on tip-toe and lightly brushed her lips across his. 'Yes, Chance, I-I agree. It's best if you go now. And please be careful. I mean, that Wylie worries me.'

'Don't let it bother you. I can handle him.'

They said their reluctant good-nights and he made his way back towards the livery, muttering to himself about all the crazy bad luck that had brought Cartwright walking in like that and getting the wrong idea.

He was thinking about it too deeply. Didn't see the two dark shadows detach themselves from the darker shadows of the corrals behind the livery. He heard a footfall, began to turn — and then the fists hammered at him, thudding into his body, one skidding along his jaw, putting him down.

The first boot driving into his ribs incensed him and he rolled swiftly, grabbed the leg, cutting a finger on a spur rowel, and heaved. The man staggered — right into the path of his companion. As they tangled, Benbow got to his feet, tasting blood and anger.

The second man regained his balance fast and thrust his pardner aside, dodging Benbow's fist and coming up inside his guard. He tried to butt Chance in the face and Benbow twisted aside, brought down an elbow on to the top of the man's head. The man grunted and his legs buckled. He clawed at Benbow for support but his arm was punched aside by a numbing blow and he fell sprawling, just as the first man roared in, swearing.

Benbow recognized the voice: Bill Redmond, the D-C ramrod. He must have brought in the bulls with Cartwright and the other ranny and Dave, angry at having found Ivy and Chance in what he figured were compromising circumstances, had set both men to wait for Benbow.

The anger bit deep now and he parried Redmond's swing, clipped the man with an uppercut that sent him staggering back. Benbow took one long stride forward, hammered four or five rapid blows into his thick midriff. Bill was a heavy man in his late thirties, not as tall as Benbow, but hard and well experienced in brawling.

He turned aside as Benbow threw a straight right and yelped as the knuckles skimmed his ear. But he knew enough to ignore the pain, clamped his arm over Benbow's, trapping it, lifted a knee towards the tall man's groin. Benbow turned enough to take the blow on his thigh, tried to wrench his right arm free but couldn't. He glimpsed the dull flash of Redmond's teeth as the man bared them, hooked him in the lower ribs, brought the same fist up to pound into Benbow's face.

Chance's head snapped back and his arm slid almost free as Bill Redmond moved his own body so as to put more force into his punches. Chance kicked him in the shins and Bill howled, started to reach down instinctively — and met Benbow's knee on the way up. The ramrod sailed back, arms flailing, one hitting his companion, who was lumbering back into the fight now.

They cussed each other and Benbow followed through, sledging a fist into the side of the cowhand's neck, hearing it strike like a cleaver thudding into a side of beef. The man folded, gagging. Redmond whirled, head down, charging in, arms spread to encircle Benbow, who was no longer where the ramrod thought he was. He tried to stop his forward motion but it was Benbow who stopped it. He thrust a leg between the ramrod's and Bill Redmond yelled as he went down, clawing at an upright corral post to keep from falling all the way.

Benbow grabbed the man's head and slammed his face solidly into the post, twice. Bill made a moaning sound as he slid to the ground in a heap. The cowhand was pushing up on one arm and Benbow, gasping for breath, ribs hurting, kicked him in the head. He fell like a poled steer.

Benbow leaned against the corral for a few minutes, head hanging, getting back his breath. Then he stumbled to the livery washbench and scooped cooling water over his throbbing, bleeding face.

*   *   *

Before Benbow quit town at sunup, aching and sore and yawning from lack of sleep, Jimmy Tuttle came shuffling across the yard, hat in hand. He was in his fifties and had worked for the Cartwright family for years, first on the ranch, then after a bad round-up accident, Dave found work for him as yardman at the general store.

'Chance, I never meant for you to get in trouble last night. Was just puttin' the tarp over your goods in your buckboard when Big Dave came in. He asked was Ivy in and I said 'yes', in the back of the store with you . . .'

'It's OK, Jim. Might've cleared the air some.'

Jim looked relieved but wondered how Benbow could act so casual with all those bruises and cuts.

Chance didn't want Ivy to see him all marked up like that. She would demand an explanation. He wouldn't lie to her but saw no point in letting her know her father had been the cause of his injuries.

In the old buckboard, the springs of which were virtually non-existent, it was going to be a long, rough and uncomfortable journey back to his cabin.

★ ★ ★

Ivy, red-eyed from tossing and turning all night, was cooking bacon and eggs, desultorily, when her father stomped into the kitchen. He still looked angry.

'By Godfrey, you think twice — no, think a dozen times! — about marryin' that damn drifter!'

Defiantly, feeling her own anger rising at his attitude, she said, 'I don't have to think about it at all, Dad! It's what I want to do — what I'm *going* to do.'

'Not as long as I have a say in it!'

'Dad! We've had this same argument for years, with every man who asked me to a dance or to go riding — '

Cartwright held up a big hand. 'All right — I may've been a mite . . . picky, but this is different.'

She sighed, turned an egg over in the sizzling grease. 'How is it different? Chance has more to offer me than any of the others. He's a steady man now he's done his drifting and is ready to settle down.'

'Not with you. I want you to come with me.'

'I'm about to have breakfast.'

'Never mind that. Come with me and see what you think of your knight in shining armour when you see what he did to Bill Redmond and Harve Gore.'

Ivy frowned. 'What? What d'you mean?'

'He fought with them after leaving here last night — nearly crippled them both! Bill won't be able to work for a couple of weeks at least — broken nose, busted teeth, eyes so swollen he can't see — '

'Good God!'

'And Harve has concussion and maybe a broken jaw. This is the kind of man you want to marry?'

She set the skillet on to the cast-iron cooling rack and turned to her father, hands on hips now, mouth tight. Big Dave took a step back hurriedly.

'You set them on Chance, didn't you? After you left here you told them to wait somewhere and to beat him up!'

There was a hint of a lift to one side of her mouth. 'Chance was too good for them and now you're trying to turn it around and blame everything on him.'

He glared, breathing hard. 'It's time he was taught a lesson!'

'Then you'd best choose someone good enough to do it — if you can find them.' She shook her head slightly. 'I'm not too concerned about Bill and Harve: they're both brawlers and have no doubt been hurt worse. If anyone's to blame, dear Father, it's you!'

He almost snorted and his big hands clenched as he glared. He shook a finger close to her face, startling her; he hadn't done that since she was a child. 'You are not yet into your majority, girl! Don't you forget that!'

He swung abruptly and strode out, letting the kitchen door swing behind him.

Ivy was shaking, she hated these rows with her father. Sometimes she hated *him* but deep down she knew it was only Big Dave's way of doing what he saw as 'best' for her.

She knew he genuinely cared for her, but wished he had a better way of showing it.

Then she thought about Benbow and smiled slowly. It took a darn good man to best Bill Redmond — and to take on Harve Gore at the same time — and win!

She would be proud to call such a man 'husband'.

★ ★ ★

It was two days after Benbow arrived back at the cabin when Wylie, up the sapling ladder and fitting fresh-cut shingles on to one end of the sloping roof, over spread tarpaper, called to Benbow.

Chance was emptying the sawpit of accumulated, compacted sawdust which came halfway to his knees, readying the pit for cutting planks from more felled lodgepole pines, with the big, vertical two-handed saw. He thought he heard Wylie call, set down the shovel, glad of the excuse for even a moment's rest from the back-breaking, sweltering chore. 'You say somethin', Wylie?'

'Visitor coming. A woman.'

Benbow dropped the shovel and clambered out of the pit, looking like something from a child's nightmare: plastered with damp sawdust, bearded with it, clothes covered with layers of it; he was more like a man-bear than anything else.

'You'll have time to wash up in the creek,' Wylie called down. 'She's riding up to the ford.'

Benbow's already thudding heart seemed to slam harder against his ribs: *it could be Ivy!* She always used the ford, never liked swimming her horse across the deep part.

He was already moving towards the creek, skirting the bushes that had screened it from his sight. Yes! It was Ivy, riding her sorrel with the pale mane and tail. She waved and he waved back as he threw himself into the water and did his best to remove the clinging sawdust and grit. It had worked between his collar and his neck, rubbed the skin raw, and the water stung.

He heard her horse splashing across the ford and minutes later she rounded the bushes, the sorrel's legs dark and wet three parts of the way up.

'I wondered what kind of a hairy monster was running around your camp,' she greeted him, but, although she smiled, he detected a tenseness around her mouth. She glanced quickly towards the cabin — and at Wylie, still up the ladder, a couple of shingles in his hands.

'You're making good progress, Chance!' She was obviously pleased. 'And I see your bruises are fading!' She laughed lightly and added, 'I take it that's Wylie up the ladder?'

'Come and meet him. He's a damn fine worker and doesn't complain, though that back wound must still be hurting plenty.'

He stopped as he made to take the bridle and she said, 'Wait, Chance. It's because of him that I'm here.'

He frowned. She seemed nervous now.

'I — don't suppose I had any right but — I thought his behaviour as you described it seemed — strange. I was already worried about you after Dad setting Bill Redmond and Harve on you — '

'So he told you. Blamed me?'

'Of course, I-I worried that he might send over some of the other men. He was very angry at what you did to Bill and Harve.'

Benbow said nothing and his expression gave nothing away about his thoughts.

'Well, the long and short of it is, I — sent a wire to Wells Fargo in Socorro.' He stiffened and his eyes narrowed some as they steadied on her face, but he didn't speak. 'Just said, 'Wylie safe. Robbers subdued'. The reply came back: 'Who's Wylie? No employee by that name'.' She paused, waiting for his reaction.

Benbow was looking up at the cabin now where Wylie was setting the wooden shingles into place. He watched for a few moments longer, turned to look at Ivy.

'I was tempted to send just such a wire myself — but I gave him my word I wouldn't.'

'Don't you think it's — strange? To say the least!'

'Let's go see what he has to say.'

Her mouth gaped as he started up towards the house in his sodden clothes. She set the sorrel after him. 'Chance! Be careful! If — if there is something wrong about this . . . '

'He doesn't wear a gun when he's working.'

Wylie had seen them coming and backed down the ladder, waiting for them, smiling and touching a hand to the brim of the old hat Benbow had found for him.

'Ma'am.' His eyes narrowed some as he studied her.

'This is Miss Ivy Cartwright, Wylie — '

'You're gonna have a fine home here, ma'am. Benbow and me are making it a fine place to live — and raise a family. He's a mighty lucky man. I didn't realize *how* lucky till now.' He turned on a charmng smile that Benbow hadn't seen before; the man was stricken!

Ivy had dismounted now and was aware of Wylie looking at her legs and figure in the denim trousers. She was aware of Benbow's regard, as well, and felt herself flush a little. 'I'm sure it's going to be just fine.' She slipped a hand under Benbow's wet left arm. 'But then, even a cave would be just fine, as long as Chance and I were married.'

Wylie sobered some, then smiled. 'You're a romantic, Ivy, but that's understandable.'

'And what do I call you? I don't know your first name.'

'Oh, I have one — not very interesting. Everyone just calls me

'Wylie'. Suits me.'

'Doesn't your boss at Wells Fargo use your first name?' asked Benbow. Wylie frowned slightly, looking from one to the other now.

'Usually it's just 'Wylie'. Sometimes, 'You Damn Fool Wylie', and even, now and again, 'Good Work Wylie' . . . ' He flicked his gaze from one to the other. 'Someone's been curious about me, I figure.'

Caught off-guard, Ivy was a little flustered but Benbow chipped in and explained what had happened.

Wylie smiled crookedly. 'Well, what d'you expect? I'm s'posed to be working under cover. They aren't about to admit they employ me and blow me into the open.'

Ivy's white teeth tugged at her bottom lip. She looked a little helplessly at Benbow.

'I still wonder why you haven't sent some sort of message, Wylie. You've wound up the deal, haven't you?'

'Between us, you and me, we've

killed most of the gang, but I haven't recovered the strongbox yet.' Wylie was very sober now. 'Like you, Chance, when I do a job, I aim to do it thoroughly, and long as that strongbox is missing . . . ' He shrugged. 'OK? You feel better now?' He flicked his gaze, accompanied by a small, winning smile, at Ivy Cartwright. '*Both* of you?'

They showed their embarrassment and Wylie's smile widened as he looked steadily at Ivy. 'Hope you feel better about me now, Ivy. Well, best get on. I see a few clouds gathering over the mountain.'

But first he went to the overhang where they had their bedrolls and gear. They saw him take a long swig from the big water canteen, then rummage around his bedroll.

When he came back and started to climb the ladder, Wylie was wearing Casey's old six-gun on the bullet belt.

4

Hardcases

Four days later the hardcases rode in. Three of them forking trail-grimed mounts, the men looking as badly marked by long and hard riding as their horses.

It was late afternoon, and Benbow and Wylie were lifting rough-cut planks, which they had sawn in the pit, into a stack higher than their heads. It swayed a little but they intended to be using the planks almost right away.

'Looks about as tottery as I feel,' Wylie opined, gasping.

Covered in sawdust and sweat, weary to the point of staggering from the truly hard work of using the pitsaw, they stopped, grabbing a moment's welcome rest.

Benbow, mopping his sweating face,

was the first to notice the trio, lined up along the edge of the brush between the cabin and the creek, downslope. He wasn't wearing a six-gun, rarely did when working, but he always kept one and a rifle within reasonable reach. He glanced at the Winchester now where it slanted in the shadow of a small stack of empty boxes, the Colt underneath with the cartridge belt wrapped around it; he was a good six long strides away.

Wylie had given up wearing Casey's six-gun on the job but he kept it handy, draping the cartridge belt and holster over any nearby bush or some implement, or even a projecting part of the cabin.

'You picked a good spot, mister.' The rider who spoke was wide of shoulder, narrow of hip and had small, darting eyes. His beard was like a fringe around his jaw, no moustache. His big hands were now folded on the saddle horn — the universal frontier sign of friendly intentions. The other two, one tall and beanpole lean, the third man slightly shorter but flabby around the middle, were just as trail dirty as their pard but they both held rifles across their thighs, watched Benbow and Wylie with narrowed eyes.

'Seems like a good spot,' Benbow agreed slowly. 'Not for sale, if you were thinking of making an offer.'

The fringe-bearded man laughed, lifted one hand and slammed it down on top of the other still gripping the saddle horn. The lean one frowned but the flabby one grinned.

'We got us a comedian, Turk!'

'We-ell, guess we can do with a laugh, after all the ridin' we done to get here,' Turk admitted, both hands now gripping the saddle horn. 'Say — I know you, fella?'

This last was directed at Wylie who was hanging back in the shadow of the stack of planks. 'Dunno. But I don't know you.'

'Aw, Slim, you hear that tone? This fella's not friendly like good old Chuckles there with his 'make an offer'.

You know, I think we got us a hostile here.'

Benbow tensed a little. *Army talk!* It was army practice to refer to Indians or Mexican renegades as 'hostiles'. These could be deserters: they looked desperate enough. He turned his head, asked quietly, 'You ever in the army, Wylie?'

The man glared, mouth tight, eyes as hard as Benbow had ever seen them. 'Long time ago.' The words were curt and spoken roughly: no encouragement to expand on the answer. Wylie shifted his wary gaze to Turk. 'You remind me of a top sergeant I once knew — a real sneaky son of a bitch, was kicked out of the army and lucky not to've been hanged for some of the stuff he pulled. Robbin' his own men, stealing from army stores, selling guns to Mexes and outlaws. Name of Reece Turkell. Any kin of yours?'

'Easy!' Benbow said. 'These boys are trouble.'

'I'll accomodate 'em. Just stay quiet, Chance. It's me they want.'

Benbow looked sharply at him, frowning. 'You can explain that later — if there is a later.'

'There will be.'

'What you two girls whisperin' about over there?' asked Turk, his tone bantering but his face suspicious and cold. He also had a look of quiet confidence on his ugly face; he knew who held the upper hand here.

'Just deciding which of you we're gonna kill first,' Wylie said, startling Benbow.

'For Chris'sakes, man!'

'We gotta *move*, Chance!'

Still speaking the last word, Wylie dived for his sixgun, hooking an arm through the looped cartridge belt, but his boots skidded on the thick layer of woodchips and he stumbled, began to sprawl.

Benbow moved the moment Wylie started his dive. He lunged for his Winchester and Colt. Wylie managed to stop from falling all the way, hands groping and thrusting at the ground, but the gunbelt slid down his arm, entangling, and he knew it was all over as he rolled on to his back, still struggling to free the Colt.

Benbow's hand had almost touched his rifle stock when the first bullet kicked jagged wood splinters into his face. He instinctively clawed at his eyes, jerking, his head striking the heavy planks on the bottom of the pile, stunning himself momentarily.

Still dazed, blinking, he made another attempt to grab the rifle but checked as he saw the trio, Turk and the skinny man and their overweight pard, menacing with their rifles; none of the weapons was smoking . . .

Turk was still sitting his saddle, though one hand was on his Colt's butt, the other holding the reins, ready to get his mount moving in a hurry. He seemed to be looking beyond Benbow and Wylie as he called,

'Don't shoot 'em! Not yet.'

That was when they heard the clash of Winchester levers and the ratcheting click of Colt hammers.

Benbow turned his head sharply, wiped a hand over his blurred eyes. There were four more men, sitting jaded mounts upslope behind them: they must have worked around and over the ridge between the cabin and the first rise of the mountain while the trio held their attention.

Caught between seven menacing guns now, Benbow and Wylie had little choice — unless bent on suicide, and neither was that way inclined.

Benbow struggled up, hands half-raised. Wylie resignedly let his six-gun rig fall and clambered to his feet, lifting his hands, too. His face was taut and pale, missing the aggression that had been there when he had faced down and sassed Turk a few minutes earlier.

'Howdy, Link. Long time, no see, huh?'

The man who spoke sat a black horse whose mane held dead leaves and twigs. Benbow figured that he and his pards had cut through the heavy brush he had aimed to dig out before moving in — it was too close to the cabin in case of fire. Now it had given cover to these gunmen. He glanced at Wylie.

'Link?'

'For 'Lincoln'. Now you know why I don't like my name, me being a dyed-in-the-wool son of the South, from Georgia. My damn stepfather was a Yankee; he named me.'

That was more information than Wylie had imparted since his arrival. Benbow wondered why the man had been candid at such a time as this.

'If we'd never met again, Moss,' Wylie was saying now, 'it would've been too soon.'

The man on the black smiled crookedly. 'Not soon enough for me. This must be Benbow.' When he got no acknowledgement, he set the black walking down slowly. His two sidekicks closed in from the sides, and the first visitors made their way up the slope. In moments, Benbow and Wylie were standing within a wide semicircle of mounted riders, every one looking capable of killing them between heart-beats without turning a hair.

The man on the black was average size, about Benbow's age, stubbled, but not enough to hide entirely his thrusting lantern jaw. He had stony eyes, like featureless pebbles, a lot colder than those of the others. Long dark hair hung raggedly from beneath his battered hat. He raked those eyes over Benbow, drifted his gaze to Wylie.

'Heard Casey tried to cut himself in. What happened to him?'

'Guess he died. I don't know nothing about him.' Wylie was deadpan as he lied, his voice with just the suggestion of anxiety. 'Benbow's not in this. You can see what he's interested in.' He gestured vaguely to the cabin. 'Got himself a real fine woman. Let him go. I'll come with you and — '

Moss snorted. 'You know better'n that.'

Wylie shrugged. 'Worth a try. He's been decent to me.'

'Then he's just another sucker. I always heard you was hard, Link, colder'n a witch's tit in midwinter.'

'Have my moments.'

'Yeah! *Had* 'em! You ain't got too many more left.'

Wylie said nothing but Benbow thought he paled a little more.

'What's goin' on here, Wylie?'

'*Wylie?*' echoed Moss. 'I never heard you use that name before.'

'Lots of things you've never heard about me.'

'Well. Don't matter at this stage, do it? You know what we want — and what we'll do to get it.'

Wylie sighed, aware of the bleakness in Benbow now, but he didn't look directly at the man.

'Told you weeks ago you was barkin' up the wrong tree.'

'Might've even believed you for a spell. Now I know different — and I want things put straight.'

'I dunno how. Nothing more I can tell you. You should've asked Collins.'

Moss laughed, harsh and brief. 'You made sure I couldn't, killin' Collins so damn quick.'

'If I'd been any slower, I'd be dead.'

'We-ell, mebbe you just postponed things a little, Link, ol' pard. 'Course, we'll have to talk to you first,' Moss swung his stony gaze to Benbow, 'or your pard.'

'He's not in this, I tell you. I was backshot when I rode in and he doctored me.'

Moss looked around the building site. 'An' here you are — workin' as a carpenter! Don't gimme that, Link! You just been hidin' out here — but someone slipped up, sendin' that wire to Wells Fargo in Socorro. You know we got friends there. Din' take too long to track you down. Everyone in Loma Vista knows there's a stranger workin' for this Benbow.'

Wylie looked thoughtful, aware of Benbow, and studiously ignoring him. But Benbow wasn't going to let it go so easily.

'Seems you and me've got to have a talk, Wylie.'

Wylie turned to look squarely at him. 'Sorry this has happened, Chance.'

'Still apologizing! Hardly counts, does it?'

'I mean it. Last thing I wanted was for you to get caught up in this. Thought I could help get the cabin finished for you and Ivy before lightin' out.' He gave a crooked smile. 'Now I've met her, I envy the hell outa you! Wish we were building the cabin for me — and someone like Ivy. But I guess it's a little late for that.'

'Who the hell are these rannies?'

'Best you dunno. Just believe me when I say they're killers.'

'Soon to be *rich* killers,' Moss dropped in coldly. 'Right, Link?'

'Wrong.' Wylie didn't elaborate beyond that and Benbow pursed his lips, wondering how come Wylie sounded so confident.

They were under seven guns, held by men ready and willing to use them.

Their own guns were on the ground, almost at their feet, but might as well be at the bottom of the deepest part of the creek, because these *hombres* wouldn't give them a chance to get to them.

'Let's get this movin' along, Moss,' growled Turk. 'We start with Benbow, mess him up big. I reckon Link'll talk fast enough then. He's all mush inside.'

'Reckon again,' Wylie said and gave Benbow a crooked smile as the man snapped his head around. 'Sorry, Chance.'

'What the hell do they want to know?'

'Location of the strongbox taken from the Tularosa stage, near Alamogordo, couple months back.'

'Heard of that. Feeney and Dekker, were they in it?'

'They were in it — but Moss here and his crew double-crossed 'em.'

'Keep talkin', Link. You might tell us what we want before you know it!'

Wylie's smile was twisted. 'Just keep looking for that first pig flying by, Moss.

When you see him, tell me. That's when you'll know as much as I do.'

Moss's stubbled face suddenly got a lot uglier and he brought up his rifle, anger flaring.

Benbow lunged sideways into Wylie, knocking him aside as the rifle blasted. Splinters flew from the high stack of planks and next moment, Benbow yelled, '*Push*!'

He threw his weight against the rickety stack. Wylie could move fast when he wanted and he hit the planks a few feet from Benbow. The stack began to topple, the long, two-inch-thick planks sliding and starting to fly through the air with minds of their own — wooden blades of death.

They slid and spun and fell, striking on one end and then falling to one side or bouncing over like trees ripped out by a hurricane wind — all in the direction of Moss and his men. The others, Turk's trio, weren't waiting to see when some of the hurtling missiles would come in their direction.

They spurred their mounts out of the way, the planks thrumming now as they fell through the air, began to slide down the slope. Two horses had their legs swept from under them and the riders yelled in terror as they fell. One went down, impaled on the untrimmed end of a plank. The other threw up an arm and had it snapped like a dead twig as he tumbled and rolled, trying to get out of the path of the sliding timber.

Turk wheeled his frightened horse across the slope, managing to get clear of the danger zone, before swinging back, eyes wide, watching. Slim and the overweight ranny had managed to get clear but Moss's lantern jaw was all askew now, the stubble soaked with blood. There was no sign of his horse.

Benbow snatched up his guns, on the side of the stack away from the direction of the fall. Someone was riding fast below, shooting without sighting. Benbow dropped to one knee, Winchester whipping to his shoulder. He triggered almost instantly and the man lurched in the saddle, dropping his gun, snatching at the saddle horn. He grasped it but he had been hammered way over to the side by Benbow's bullet and his upper body flailed and smashed through the brush as he fought to stay in the saddle of his panicked mount.

Benbow was down on his belly now, rifle sweeping, whip-cracking shot after shot. Wylie's six-gun was thundering, too, his hand moving it in a long arc as he tracked a rider going up over the crest. The Colt bucked as he got off his last shot. The rider kept going but the horse's rump swayed and twitched as it carried the man over the crest and out of sight.

Dust was everywhere, tendrils of gunsmoke drifting through it. Benbow was filthier than ever, as was Wylie who was reloading his Colt. They stood side by side, each facing a different direction, looking at the chaos they had caused as the last couple of planks slid into the bushes at the foot of the slope, near bodies of men and at least one downed horse.

'Hell, now we gotta stack all them damn planks up again!' Wylie said grumpily, but when Benbow looked at him sharply, he grinned through all the dirt.

'Sure, *Link*. But first we have to talk. Plain and square.'

Casually, by accident or design, the barrel of his rifle swung in Wylie's direction. His grin faded quickly.

5

Clay Pigeon

The man with the busted arm and the one Benbow had almost blown out of the saddle were still alive. But the latter was in bad shape, ripped up from belly to scalp by his rough passage through the brush. They were propped up in the shade with water to hand but neither was conscious. A dead man and one horse lay more to the left, the man being the overweight ranny who had first appeared with Turk.

Moss had disappeared.

Benbow stood, rifle in his left hand, right hand not far from his holstered Colt. Wylie waited there, under the other's hard stare, aware that it was time for coming clean.

'Seven of 'em — and they scattered like chaff in a wind. Sure, they took a few shots, but why the hell did they run instead of standin' to fight us?'

Wylie pointed and Benbow saw for the first time the almost straight-up narrow column of smoke rising from the top of the mountain.

'Lookout. Must've seen something, warned 'em with the smoke.'

'Christ, Wylie! How many men've you got after you?'

'Ten or a dozen — that's what they started with, anyway, but we're slowly whittlin' 'em down.'

'It's no longer 'we'. I want to know what the hell is going on. Starting with what did that lookout see?'

Wylie shrugged, uncomfortable. 'Maybe a cavalry column.'

'Don't get many of them out here — but leave that. I want to know who the hell you really are and why so many want to kill you.'

They sat on a log and rolled cigarettes. Wylie was aware that Benbow kept his rifle right alongside, resting against his thigh. He lit up, smiled faintly.

'I am a Wells Fargo agent. That strong-box I mentioned earlier contained over twenty-five thousand dollars' worth of gold.'

Benbow arched his eyebrows at that. 'Helluva lot to risk on a stage run.'

'That's what they figured everyone would think — that no one would risk that much in a stagecoach. But you think about it: what else can you do out here? No railroads, army forts scattered to hell an' gone. You need somethin' in a hurry, it has to be by good old Wells Fargo.'

'Yeah. I heard it said once that that's how they got started. Carried stuff where no one else would risk it, through Injun lands or known outlaw country.'

'That's true. But they did it not so much by big teams of armed men ridin' shotgun, as everyone thought, but by using decoys. Fake stage runs, all the trimmings to make it look like they were carrying the Federal Treasury or something just as valuable. Real stuff went by another route, sometimes in a wagon under some ranch gear, other times sittin' in the stage boot with luggage.'

'That must've been a helluva risk!'

Wylie smiled. 'Some — but the passengers weren't always just . . . passengers. You know what I mean?'

Benbow thought for a moment, then nodded. 'Special agents posing as drummers or ordinary folk payin' their way.' Wylie nodded. 'You . . . ?'

'That's my job — escort. 'Clay pigeons' they call us in the Company. But that's only if someone breaks our cover and makes us a target.'

'And you were the escort on the Tularosa-Alamogordo run?'

Wylie dragged on his cigarette and studied the glowing tip. He nodded. 'Was a little different. I went under cover, joined up with Moss Ryan's outfit, posing as a man on the run. We heard he was gathering a larger wild bunch than usual to get this strongbox. He knew somethin' about the decoys, too, which was what made the boss decide to send me under cover: to go join 'em, see if I could find the leak — and head off a slaughter if I could. Wasn't easy.'

'Damn well dangerous, I'd say!'

'It was that. The snake who sold out and told Ryan about the decoys turned up in an outlaw camp one time when I was with 'em. He knew me. Maybe not that I was a special agent, but that I worked for Wells Fargo.'

'*That* must've been kind of exciting.'

Wylie nodded, smiled ruefully. 'You could say that. Had to shoot my way out. Too late for 'em to call off the hold-up. Feeney and Dekker and another outlaw named Silver jumped the stage. They found nothin', of course; shot up the guard and driver and got back just as I took a chance and made a run for it.' He ground out the cigarette against the log and looked straight into Benbow's face. 'They come after me, and I ended up here, with Casey's bullet in my back. After you played the good Samaritan, and took care of Casey and the other two, I figured this was a good place to hole up until all the excitement died down and Ryan got tired of looking for me.'

'Then Ivy inadvertently threw a spoke in the wheel by sending that wire to Socorro.'

'Couldn't be helped, I guess. But Ryan's got spies everywhere and once he got word about the wire — '

'Only a matter of time before his men turned up here.'

'Yeah. And by that time they must've figured no one had yet produced the strongbox, so I must be the only one knew where it was hidden.'

Benbow suddenly stood, scooping up his rifle, startling Wylie, who rolled backwards off the log, whipping up his Colt. But he held his fire.

Chance Benbow was looking down at the creek ford, which could be seen from this far up the slope. There was a large band of riders splashing across.

The sinking sun flashed from all the guns that were in their hands.

'Two of us aren't gonna drive off that many — unless you've got a cannon stashed somewhere handy.'

Wylie seemed to relax. 'That's what Moss's lookout saw from the top of the mountain.'

Benbow frowned. 'A posse?'

'Good as, mebbe better. That's my chief from Wells Fargo down there. Ivy's wire stirred up more than Ryan's outfit, I'd say.'

* * *

The Wells Fargo man's name was Sawney Tilton. He was huge, wide as a hoe-handle across the shoulders, thick as a tallow keg around the middle, with treelike legs and arms like branches. And on top of all this hugeness sat a child's head.

It looked that way to Benbow, anyway. The man's head was far too small for the rest of him and the oddness was enhanced when Tilton spoke: his voice rumbled out of his chest like rocks tumbling into a gorge.

They had 'questioned' the wounded men, learnt little, except for a general area where the outlaws might make for, or where they could disperse. Two men had been dispatched to take the wounded back to Socorro.

'If they make it,' Tilton's voice rumbled. 'If not, bury 'em and come after us.'

'Your boss is kinda tough,' opined Benbow. Before Wylie could answer Tilton said:

'You've done well, Wylie. But it's time to come back into the fold; staying under cover won't gain us anything now.' Pigeon-egg-size eyes sought Chance Benbow, squatting with a welcome tin mug of coffee close by. 'Sorry, Benbow. You're gonna lose your helper. I need him more than you do.'

'Too bad. He's a damn good carpenter. And willing.'

'Sounds like Wylie. We need you to get that strongbox from wherever you stashed it, Link.'

Wylie sobered, shifted weight from one foot to the other. 'Yeah — well, Chief, I — er — I ain't exactly sure it's where I left it.'

Tilton stiffened and there was a loud gust of air, pretty much like a hog snorting, blasting from large, hairy nostrils. 'Think I must have something stuck in my ear . . . '

'Sorry, Chief. But I sank it in a riverbend, it havin' plenty of weight to hold it down, but — '

'Judas Priest! Don't you tell me it was the Rio Hondo!' Wylie nodded silently. 'Christ! It's in flood! There was a cloudburst over the Sacramento Range, wiped out half the Mescalero reservation and washed it down into the valley. They say some renegades got away because of it. River was nearly two miles wide by the time it hit the plains.'

'That's what I heard, Chief, and why I say I'm not sure the box is still where I sank it.'

The chief sat down on the log and his

weight lifted the other end a little. Tilton pondered for a long minute, Wylie watching and waiting in silence. Then the big man said,

'This another reason why you been hiding out?'

'Yeah, Chief. I aimed to wait a mite longer, let the flood waters go down, then ride back and check the Hondo before I got in touch. Hopefully with good news.'

Tilton's fleshy face was set in taut lines. 'The best news will be when you locate that damn box.'

'It was a deep-water bend, Chief. I'm hoping I sunk it deep enough for the flood to pass over without disturbin' it too much. Maybe it just pushed it hard against the rocks instead of setting it tumbling or picking it up and carrying it away. Cross your fingers it jammed under a ledge.'

'We'll find out. I s'pose it wasn't a bad idea, hiding it that way, but . . . How long'll it take to ride to the Hondo from here?'

'Mebbe three days — if we push it a little.'

'We'll push it a lot. You, me and a few men'll go to the Hondo, the rest'll get on the trail of Ryan's scum.' He flicked his eyes towards Benbow. 'You won't be bothered by them again, Benbow. They won't come back here now. If we have any luck, only place they'll go is to Hell.'

'Like to stay and give Chance a hand to clean up some, Chief. This mess is more'n a one-man job.'

'That's what it was before you came along and helped out,' the big man rumbled flatly. 'And that's what it'll have to be now. You can call in help if you need it, can't you, Benbow?'

'I'll manage. Obliged for all you did, Wylie. Be glad to see you any time you care to drop by.'

They shook hands and Wylie nodded. 'Tell Ivy I'm sorry I'll miss the wedding. But I'll try and stop by sometime, or send a present.' Then he added; 'You're a mighty lucky man,

Chance. Ivy's a woman in a thousand.'

Benbow nodded, thinking, *Yeah, but it'll be up to Big Dave when — and if — the wedding happens* . . .

He knew that even if Ivy could talk Cartwright around, the man would impose almost impossible conditions.

But Chance Benbow would meet them — somehow. Nothing was going to keep him from marrying Ivy.

★　★　★

Progress seemed almost non-existent without Wylie. His strength and know-how had made all the difference. What rightly should have been a two-man lift took Chance hours now instead of a matter of minutes. With long planks and logs, he rigged tripods and rope slings and levers. Using the pitsaw, solo, was a quick way to a heart attack but he had no choice. He couldn't afford to hire anyone and he hadn't made any close friends in the valley.

He was used to doing things on his

lonesome and figured he had been spoiled by Wylie's enthusiasm and gratitude; he'd just have to work harder and longer hours if he wanted to meet the prove-up deadline. By the time he had finished the walls he practically had to crawl into his bedroll at night. It became a little easier after he completed laying the roof shingles. That gave him shelter, too: log walls with untrimmed or unframed cut-outs for windows and doorways, and a shingle roof above. Putting up some of the heavy planks for a ceiling was awkward, back-breaking work, though.

He was sorting planks by length when a rider came in over the mountain, his chestnut limping slightly. Benbow grabbed his rifle and was waiting with the hammer spur under his thumb when the man arrived, lifting his right hand in greeting. Benbow frowned — he had seen this man recently.

'Randy Kelso,' the man called. 'I was with the Wells Fargo posse a few days back.'

Benbow recalled him then, a young man in his twenties who, when riding out with the posse, had tossed him a full tobacco sack, with a casual wave and a grin.

He lowered the rifle but did not set it down yet. 'Howdy, Randy.' He didn't ask what the rider was doing here; he would explain soon enough. 'Wylie and the others reach the Hondo yet?'

'Likely not. There's been a rockfall in the pass, due to the heavy rain up that way. We had to go the long way round. Rough as a cob, and my hoss fell, sprained a fetlock, threw me against a boulder.' He lifted his hat a little so Benbow could see the edge of a crude bandage. 'I'm OK but ol' Flyer here' — he patted the chestnut's neck as it stood, favouring the right foreleg — 'couldn't handle that rough country. Chief sent me back and Wylie suggested I could stay here and lend you a hand till the fetlock rests some more. There's plenty of men to handle Ryan's bunch when they catch up with 'em.'

'Well, bless the Chief — and Wylie, too. Step on down. Put your horse in the empty corral. Be better by himself — he wouldn't get much rest in with the *remuda*.'

Randy didn't know a lot about carpentry and his work was mighty rough, but he was strong and willing, and between them they got much of the heavy work out of the way in a couple of days.

They made the doors and shutters for the windows but Benbow found he only had three iron hinges. He could make do with leather but it wouldn't be as durable and he aimed for this place to *look* permanent, because he intended that was the way it was going to be.

'Have to go into Loma Vista for hinges and screws, dammit. Might's well stock up on grub and other supplies at the same time.' Benbow looked slightly annoyed. 'My own fault. I forgot hinges last time I was in town. Coupla fellas beat me up and sort of took my mind off things. Damn! Gonna lose a coupla days now. Wanted to get started on the fireplace!'

'I dunno nothin' about fireplaces. An' you know, I ain't got much of a square eye for hangin' doors and shutters by myself: they'll likely end up crooked, leave gaps.'

'You trying to talk yourself out of a job?'

'Guess mebbe I am. You got a nice-lookin' cabin shapin' up here, Chance. I'd rather do the jobs that ain't gonna spoil it if I mess up. I can go get the hinges and stuff after we bring up the riverstones for the fireplace and you can get started layin' 'em. Won't lose any time then.'

Benbow was eager to get the fireplace built and the chimney set up. It would give the cabin the look of permanence he was striving for, inside and out. Finishing this fireplace was important to him: Ivy had often spoken of the big riverstone fireplace in the Cartwright ranch house and how much she enjoyed it during the bitter winters, when she was growing up: happy memories. He had promised she would have a good fireplace here, too — not as big, likely not as elegant as her father's, but he figured he could do a reasonable job that would please her.

'OK, Randy. I'm impatient to get started — and a mite worried that I won't make it as good as I want.'

'Hell, you're doin' a real bang-up job, Chance. I wouldn't mind livin' in a cabin like this with my woman. If I had one.'

'You go find your own woman to build one for,' Chance said with a grin, punching Randy lightly on the shoulder. 'OK, we'll bring up some more rocks from the creek and set 'em to drying before you leave.'

Randy looked at the hundred or so river rocks already spread around on the slope. 'Gotta be dry before you use 'em?'

'Sure. Wet rocks are likely to explode with the fire's heat. When I was in the cavalry, a pard of mine was blinded when one exploded.'

Randy looked sheepish. 'I'd hate to count the number of trail fires I've built with wet stones, not even thinkin' about 'em explodin'.'

Benbow nodded. 'Always possible it'll happen.'

As usual, they had commenced work as soon as there was enough light. So, after lugging more rocks up to the cabin on the crude sled, dragged by one of Benbow's horses, Randy Kelso was able to drive out just after noon, the buckboard rattling. Benbow knew he was going to have to take time off to check those axles and hubs pretty soon, too; it was a long time since they had been greased and the nuts adjusted.

He had cleared an area at the northern end of the cabin, tamped the earth down hard and firm for the fireplace. This was the direction the freezing winter winds would come from. He had planned the bedroom to be off to one side where it would get residual heat from the fireplace, through a vent he cut in the wall, after he and Ivy turned in. It was already a snug room, the only one with plank flooring, raised a little above the ground, and enclosed underneath so as to trap the warm air — and cooler air in summer. He carried in some of the larger rocks, began arranging them how he wanted them. Then he numbered each with chalk so they would match the crude sketch he had made and be placed so as to give the fireplace some kind of symmetry and style.

He knew he was probably going to spend more time than he should on this fireplace, but it had become important to him — and he wanted to please Ivy.

Just the thought of doing something special for her made him feel all kind of warm. He found he was squatting over his drawings and the first set-pieces of riverstones, looking wistfully at the planked square that would be their bedroom, imagining all the wonderful things they would do together.

He shook himself and started to manoeuvre another rock into place, rough hands shaking a little.

By God, he could hardly wait to marry that girl!

6

Death Trail

Benbow had, of course, written a short note to Ivy, and while Kelso checked the goods he had purchased against Chance's list, she turned her back and read it swiftly.

She smiled to herself as she folded the paper and slipped it into the front of her dress.

Chance Benbow, you are a wondeful man, she said to herself. *You say you haven't the words to tell me how you feel about me, but your actions speak volumes! I-I can't wait to marry you!*

Aloud, she said: 'Chance didn't mention potatoes, but I know he likes them a lot, so take a sack with you, Randy.'

'I dunno as I have enough money left to pay, ma'am.'

'Oh, that can be settled some other time.'

He hurried around the counter as she had to move some trade goods to reach the sacks of potatoes. He moved them for her without effort.

'Thank you, Randy. You're a gentleman.'

Pleased, he started carrying the purchases out to the buckboard he had parked outside. A few passers-by threw him curious looks, he being a stranger in Loma Vista. A couple of strolling cowboys slowed and leaned against the awning support, watching him arranging his load.

One had a plaster across his nose and there was dark bruising surrounding both eyes. He tended to breathe through his mouth, his lips were split and swollen.

The other man showed marks of having been in a fight, too: his jaw was badly swollen and his neck purple with bruised flesh, one eye was almost closed.

From inside the store, after serving a customer, Ivy wiped her hands down her apron and absently looked through the front window as Randy moved about the buckboard tray, settling the sacks and small nail kegs firmly, then tying them around with rope.

She stiffened as she saw the two men at the awning post, rolling cigarettes while they watched him work. She put a hand involuntarily to her mouth.

Big Bill Redmond and Harvey Gore, still looking the worse for wear after their encounter with Chance Benbow. They weren't doing anything but watch Randy, yet she felt knotted up inside. She knew these two, troublemakers, always on hand — and willing — when her father thought he needed to resort to violence or intimidation so as to get what he wanted.

She hurriedly wrote the note she had meant to give Kelso in reply to Benbow's, and went outside, not looking at Redmond and Gore.

'Oh, Randy. Give this to Chance, will

you please?' She held out the note from the edge of the boardwalk so he had to lean down, stretching close, to reach it. As he did, grinning, she said in a low voice,

'It may be nothing, but be careful of those two.' She rolled her eyes towards the D-C cowboys and Randy had enough sense not to look in their direction, just touch a hand to his hatbrim as he folded the note into his shirt pocket.

'I'll see Chance gets it, ma'am. *Adios*.'

'Safe drive back, Randy.' As she turned she let her gaze casually pass over Redmond and Gore; she nodded briefly. They touched hands to their hatbrims, but were more interested in Randy's departure.

He wasn't all that used to buckboards, and he fouled some of the passing traffic, earning some blistering curses. It seemed to amuse Gore and he laughed out loud.

'Think we got us a greenhorn here, Bill.'

'Yeah. He could come to grief on his way back to Benbow's on that narrow trail that skirts Breechblock Canyon if he's not careful.'

'Mebbe we better follow on behind and make sure nothin' happens to him, huh?'

'Harve, I didn't think you could be so kind and considerate. What a good idea.'

Chuckling, they started towards the hitchrack outside the saloon as Randy weaved his way down the street.

Ivy's anxious face was pale against her drapery display in the front window of the store as she watched, helpless to prevent the trouble she was sure was coming.

★   ★   ★

Chance Benbow stepped back from the fireplace, pressing his hands hard into his lower back as he admired his handiwork.

'Not bad — not bad at all,' he

allowed. ''Course, the light favours things and covers up my mistakes.'

He frowned suddenly. *The light!* Hell, it was getting late, heading towards sundown. Concentrating on shaping the fireplace according to his plan, laying and working the heavy stones into position, he hadn't noticed the passing of the hours.

He thought Randy would have been back by this. Randy knew Benbow would be needing those sacks of cement . . .

He walked to the doorway of the cabin.

Could Randy have gotten himself lost? Not likely, not if he was a rider for Wells Fargo. Still, he had said he wasn't used to handling buckboards and their teams.

Benbow hadn't eaten since breakfast and he washed up in the creek, aiming to grab some cold grub and ride back along the trail a ways. Of course, it was possible Randy was running late and had stayed over in town rather than tackle the trail back to the valley at night, especially the narrow one that ran round the high rim of Breechblock Canyon.

Drying his face and upper body on an old floursack, Benbow looked up sharply as he heard horses, and felt the relief flooding through him.

He hadn't realized how tense he was.

But it wasn't the buckboard rattling its way to the ford: there were two riders, and it took but a moment to recognize Redmond and Gore across the stretch of water. He strapped on his six-gun as Bill Redmond hauled rein and waved.

'Hey, Benbow! You send someone to town in your buckboard?'

Tense again, Chance answered. 'What if I did?'

Redmond turned to Gore. 'See? Told you it looked like his buckboard.'

'Dunno how you could tell, wrecked like it was,' Gore answered, on cue from Redmond who was having trouble holding in his grin.

'Wrecked? What the hell're you talkin' about?'

'We're on our way back to D-C and noticed there'd been a fall-away or somethin' midway along the Breechblock Canyon trail. Harve looked over and saw a wrecked buckboard down there. Thought it looked like yours; you know that tailgate you spilled the yaller paint on last — '

'Any sign of the driver?'

'No, nothin'. But we din' climb down.' Redmond's voice took on a different tone, meaner, as he added, 'We still ain't fully — recovered. But figured you might like to know. Just bein' neighbourly.'

'I'm obliged.'

He heard their no-longer-controlled laughter as they waved casually and spurred off into the gathering darkness.

By then, Benbow was running towards his corrals.

★   ★   ★

Randy Kelso was dead.

Chance couldn't read the churned-up

sign on the trail very well in the dark but there was enough to tell him the buckboard had been deliberately forced off the trail.

It had slewed and bounced, and finally upended, landing on Randy and breaking his back and most every rib, as well as cracking his skull. The goods were strewn all across the slope, but Benbow paid them no heed.

The team had somehow gotten loose from the harness before the buckboard slid over the edge and were peacefully grazing, reins and bridles trailing on a patch of grass when he arrived.

There was nothing he could do for Randy, so he wrapped his broken body in the tarp used to cover the goods in the buckboard's tray, roped it around tightly. Then he clambered back up, caught the horses and rigged up his rope to the long, trailing reins on the chestnut and worked it carefully on the narrow trail, hauling Randy Kelso's body up.

It was full dark by now and stars

were studding the sky by the time he reached his valley. Working by the light of two lanterns, he dug a grave on the slope, just below the crest, and interred Kelso.

He knew few words from the Good Book and simply stood, hatless, and said, 'I'm obliged for all your help, Randy ... I'll see someone pays for this.'

In his pocket was the bloodstained note Ivy had written and given to Randy outside her store. He had taken it from Randy's torn shirt pocket and read it before climbing out of the canyon:

Chance — I hope there won't be any trouble for Randy, but Bill Redmond and Harvey Gore are outside taking an interest in him.

Thank you for your note. I love you, too. Ivy.

This would have been enough to condemn those two D-C riders, even if they hadn't been stupid enough to stop by his cabin so they could gloat and amuse themselves.

He cleaned and oiled his Winchester and Colt by lamplight inside the walls of the cabin, loaded them, filled all the loops on his cartridge belt and put a spare carton of ammunition in his saddle-bags.

With a canteen full of cold creek water and some hardtack in his grubsack he set out on the night ride to the D-C ranch.

* * *

There were lights burning in the big ranch house and the bunkhouse, the red points of cigarettes outside the latter attesting to the fact that some of the cowboys were enjoying a last smoke before turning in.

There was movement on the dark porch of the ranch house and Benbow dropped a hand to his gunbutt.

'No need for that,' called Dave Cartwright sharply. 'I fired them both as soon as I found out what they'd done. They claim they didn't mean your driver to die. The damn fools!'

'Who you talking about?' Benbow wanted to get this *right*. He didn't aim to be sent on any wild-goose chase after the wrong men.

'Redmond and Gore.' Cartwright was standing at the top of the short steps now, hatless, smoking one of his long, thick cigars he imported from some place with an exotic-sounding name. 'I don't condone wanton killing, you should know that.'

'But you don't mind setting a couple of hardcases on to someone in a dark alley.'

The cigar's red tip moved in a short, jerky arc. 'That was a spur of the moment thing — I-I oughtn't to've done it. It upset Ivy.'

Benbow felt his lips move in a crooked smile.

He'd been kind of — upset, too . . . .

'Never mind that, Dave. You talkin' gospel about firin' them snakes?'

'By God! Don't you doubt my word! I —'

'Are you talking gospel?' rapped out Benbow, interrupting. 'I don't have all damn night to consider your finer feelings. Fact, didn't know you had any.'

'Damn you! I've a good mind not to — ' The rancher stopped abruptly. 'All right. A man lost his life unnecessarily tonight. It's only right it should be squared. I paid 'em both off, so they'll have money in their pockets and they've each got a spare horse.'

'That was thoughtful of you.'

'You shut up and listen! The horses belonged to them, mustangs they'd caught and broke in, ran with my *remuda*. A lot of my hands've done the same. I'm just telling you they can outrun you and they've got money to help them.'

'They won't outrun me. And money won't help them.'

He heard Cartwright blow out a short, sharp breath.

'You must think you're damn good.'

'Where're they headed, Dave? If you're gonna help, for Chris'sakes stop pussyfooting, and tell me all you're gonna so I can get on my way.'

'Judas priest! You are an *aggravating* man, Benbow!'

'The hell with you.'

Chance started to haul his mount around and Cartwright moved down one step. 'I'm doing this as much for Ivy as I am for you! *More!* They'd head over the range, maybe to Magdalena. Harve's got kin there.'

'Keep an eye on the cabin for me,' Benbow said and spurred away into the darkness.

'Wha-at . . . ?' Cartwright came right down the steps now, just making out the moving shadow of Benbow and his mount. 'Who the . . . ?'

He jammed the cigar into his mouth and stomped back up on to the porch, went into the ranch house and slammed the door behind him.

'Think he'll ever take that Benbow

for a son-in-law?' someone still smoking on the bench outside the bunkhouse queried.

'He don't, he'll lose a daughter,' another voice answered and there were murmurings of agreement.

One way or another, it seemed to them that, at long last, Big Dave had met his match in Chance Benbow.

7

Shallow Grave

He was pretty much exhausted but the horse was fresh so he pushed on until he topped out on the mountain. The moon was pooling the sky with spreading ripples of silver light among a few scudding clouds and he decided to camp for the night.

Glancing at the sky and figuring there could be rain before morning, he searched for and found a convenient overhang on a rock ledge and spread his bedroll underneath. Too tired to eat much, he munched some hardtack, spat out most of it and washed the rest down with canteen water. He rolled back on to the blanket, tipping his hat over his eyes, groping for the rifle alongside him.

He slept almost immediately and

soundly. The sky was light but the sun hadn't yet risen properly when he awoke. He was on the trail in minutes, munching hardtack again. This time he ate it all, belly growling.

He knew the trail to Magdalena but he didn't know if he could take Dave Cartwright's word that that was the way his quarry would head. Dave might have been guessing, or deliberately throwing him off; mostly he had fired Redmond and Gore because he knew that if he didn't he would widen the gulf already there between himself and Ivy.

'Helping out' Benbow was a gesture he had to make — though Chance admitted Big Dave likely would never have sanctioned the actions of his ramrod.

The fresh trail was easy enough to follow. Cartwright's blacksmith was employed full-time, made the shoes for the large *remuda*, and stamped a small D with the hanging C on each one; pride or vanity, it didn't matter. But it sure made it easy to follow these two snakes.

And for that reason, Benbow didn't go riding hell for leather along the clear trail.

Redmond was no fool; he would realize the blacksmith's stamp on the horseshoes was the same as blazing a trail. They had spare horses with them and that would make it easy for Gore to ride ahead with both spares, messing up the trail just enough to make it look like all four horses and both riders had gone that way. While Redmond settled in behind some high point, waited for Benbow to show, following the treacherous trail, he could draw his bead at his leisure . . .

So Chance Benbow climbed his mount up a tree-clad ridge, using the timber as cover, worked to the top, then put his horse against a large tree with spreading foliage. He stood on the saddle and climbed up amongst the branches.

They screened him well and he used

the field glasses confident that no sunlight could penetrate here and flash from the lenses, giving away his intentions, if not his position.

They had had too good a start for him to expect to see any sign of them ahead as yet. So he climbed down and moved along the trail again. They had made some attempt to cover it, but he was well experienced in tracking men and their efforts barely slowed him down.

He was surprised to find where they had camped for the night: not as far along as he might have expected. They were careless; this was one place they should have covered well, for it told him plenty. He had little trouble in picking up the direction they had taken although they had laid a false trail until it became lost amongst heavy brush.

As soon as he realized it, Benbow went back to a creek he had crossed, turned upstream, hoping again that Cartwright had been right in his guess that the fugitives would make for Magdalena.

Not long after, he knew he had guessed right. Some disintegrating horse dung was caught in a tiny inlet made by the current swirl under some trailing willow tendrils that hung down to the water. The dung was still fresh enough to break up and not clump as it would, if older.

Rifle butt on his thigh, he walked his mount up the creek through the shallows. When the water deepened, wetting his dangling boots and the horse's belly, he set it closer to the bank, then, eventually, up on to solid ground.

As the animal heaved beneath him, a rifle crashed and a bullet punched air beside his right ear. He was going out of the saddle instantly, moving to the right, figuring in that split second that the gunman would compensate left. He figured correctly and the hidden rifle blazed in two fast shots as he struck the bank and rolled away from the water.

The horse knew how to take care of itself, lunged up on to solid ground and crashed into the brush, pursued by two more bullets; the bushwhacker was trying to put Benbow afoot.

Those shots gave Benbow the man's position: up a tree set back from the creek but high enough for the killer to see the watercourse and anyone coming along it.

They had outfoxed him, setting up an ambush so soon, and doing it here where a man would not expect one with so little solid cover about; brush might deflect a bullet but only by the purest luck. Most of the heavy, round-nosed .44/.40 slugs fired by the Winchesters would just plough on through, smashing any small branches in their path.

Worming his way back, Benbow held his fire. With some luck, the confusion of the horse heaving on to the bank, and water spraying, the rifleman might not have seen where he went.

When the bullet slammed past his face, sending twigs and leaves flying, he figured he had guessed wrong; that son of a bitch had eyes like a hawk. Which might mean it was Harve Gore; he was Cartwright's hunter, brought in the venison and rabbits, the occasional squirrel and bird, when it was time for a break from the monotony of beef.

It would be like Redmond to set up Gore with this chore. He wouldn't wait around to make sure Harve was successful, but would use the time to put a lot of distance between himself and Benbow, just in case Gore lost the deal.

Again he saw the puff of gunsmoke almost halfway up the tree; the bullet came crashing through the brush over his head. While Gore was briefly blinded by the surging cloud of powder smoke Chance made his move: he rolled back into the creek, bellied along, using elbows and knees through the chill water and mud of the bank under the overhanging bushes. They didn't provide much cover, and no protection at all from bullets, but if Gore hadn't spotted him . . .

He dropped flat, face in the muddy water, as the rifle whiplashed again. He heard the bullet tearing up the brush where he had been a few moments before, grinned tightly, and crawled along for another five yards. Gore made several more shots and Benbow could tell the man was getting rattled now, had realized his target must have moved, and was shooting wild, randomly.

Good. That would help throw his aim off.

Time to get on to solid ground again. He crawled out under an overhang of heavy foliage, snaking through the dead leaves and twigs, doing his best not to shake the branches above. He glanced back twice, changed direction slightly. The crack of Gore's Winchester was closer now. Benbow was not quite opposite the killer's tree but he was a lot closer than earlier and at an angle he could use.

Breathing steadily but deeply, fighting the urge to sneeze as dust prickled his nostrils, Benbow carefully eased some leafy branches aside, enough so he could see across the creek.

He found Gore's tree easily; the man was shooting faster and more wildly now as he realized he did not know where Benbow was, merely hoping his lead would find a target.

He found out his mistake in the next few seconds, though maybe it happened too fast for it to register in the man's brain.

Benbow exploded out of the brush, head and shoulders thrusting up violently through the branches covering him. The curve of the rifle butt was already clamped against his right shoulder, the lever working.

Three fast shots cracked out, rolling into one long roar across the creek. Leaves and twigs and bark ripped from Gore's tree and then the man himself appeared, tumbling through his screening foliage, rifle falling from fingers that had for ever lost their strength. The body bounced from branch to branch, loose and without direction — except down.

Benbow heard him thud to the ground, saw the layer of dead leaves erupt. A few drifted away on the wafting of a breeze. Cartridge in the hot chamber, finger on the trigger, eyes still sighting down the barrel, Benbow held his rifle on Gore's body, which he could see through the bushes.

No movement.

He waited.

Still no movement.

He waded across, holding the rifle clear of the water when it deepened to his chest, and found Gore would never move again of his own volition. His face and upper chest were smashed in, first by the bullets, completed by his fall across branches of the tree that had sheltered him.

Now all he had to do was find Bill Redmond.

★ ★ ★

Redmond came to Benbow.

The ramrod knew the sound of Harvey Gore's rifle, it was a .44./40, but Gore had short-loaded for hunting smaller game, so he didn't destroy too much meat, or the pelt in cases where he knew he could sell it for profit.

The rifle made a flatter sound, as if cut off by some intervening wall or obstacle. It didn't echo, slapping around the trees and ridges like a normal Winchester shot.

But the sound carried just the same and Redmond, up in the high country, a mile or so upstream, heard the gunfight clearly.

He concentrated on the difference in the sounds of the rifles. Gore was doing most of the shooting, then it became more random, short bursts of three or four shots.

The D-C foreman swore. 'Damn you, Harve! You've let him rattle you! You'll never find target shootin' up the countryside that way!'

Then he heard the rapid fire of

Benbow's rifle and listened with tightening mouth as the echoes slapped and rolled around the ridges.

There was no answering fire from Gore and he knew, as surely as if he had witnessed it, that Harve had been shot out of his tree.

'Goddamn you, Harve! You were a fine shot, but you was always short on brains! Now *I*'ve got to go down and finish the job!'

It wasn't anything he looked forward to, but as he checked his guns, mouth suddenly dry, he knew he had a chance this way, by going back to meet Benbow. The man wouldn't be expecting it, and that was a mighty good thing, as far as Bill Redmond was concerned.

* * *

Chance Benbow was burying Harve Gore's body when Redmond arrived.

Having spent so many years in the wilderness and seen the results of bodies left lying out overnight where predatory animals prowled — and that was just about *anywhere* in this country — he felt no man needed the extra indignity of passing through an animal's digestive system after death.

He had sharpened a stake as thick as his arm and the creek-bank soil was easy to dig. He made a shallow grave, about six feet by two, but only just over two feet deep. He used pieces of bark stripped from one of the nearby trees to remove the loosened soil from the hole.

As he bent to scrape up some dirt, Redmond fired his first shot. Benbow let himself fall full length and reddish-black earth kicked over him, a little gravel mixed with it stinging his neck. He didn't have to think about who might be taking a shot at him or why. He reached up over the edge for his rifle where he had left it. The second bullet burned across the back of his hand but he had already been tugging the weapon towards him and it fell into the grave with him.

It was cramped and he didn't realize that his head showed above the edge until a bullet sent his hat flying. His scalp tingled as he knelt, trying to see past the heap of loose earth he had flung out.

'Just stay right where you are, Benbow! It'll save me some work! All I'll have to do is shovel in the dirt on top of you!'

'There'll be room for you, Bill!'

Redmond rose up on his piece of high ground for a better shot and Benbow saw his hat and the point of one shoulder. He beaded and fired faster than a snake strikes and Redmond yelled, as much in surprise as pain, as the lead seared his shoulder. It sent him tumbling and he slid down to where his horse stood, tensed with ears pricked.

Benbow stood and slammed two more shots at him. One tore the rifle from Bill's hand and splinters drove into his flesh. Startled, hurt twice in a couple of seconds, he gave an involuntary whine and leapt for the saddle. As he rose up and swung his leg across, he drew his Colt, twisted his body and triggered.

Benbow, just climbing out of the grave, reared back, blinded by flying dirt. Redmond's horse whinnied and spun, almost unseating him. But now he was mounted, he could see Benbow in the grave, struggling to clear his eyes. With a wild whoop, he drove home the spurs, fought the reins with his blood-slippery hand and leaped the horse down the slope.

Benbow threw himself back as the horse thundered in. Redmond was leaning far out of the saddle now, Colt aimed downwards. As the horse jumped over the open grave, Bill fired and Benbow was slammed back hard. His head struck the side and dirt spilled down inside his shirt. He had twisted somehow and his left arm was trapped under him as Redmond wheeled and thundered back, face alive with savage excitement.

Benbow fired the rifle one-handed,

butt braced into his side. It almost jumped from his grip. He wrenched his left arm out from beneath him and fumbled for the lever. But his arm was numb, useless. In any case, another shot was unnecessary. His bullet had driven up through Redmond, entering between his lower ribs and angling through his torso, tearing up his lungs and heart.

His body fell hard, bounced off the pile of dirt at one side, then slid down on top of Benbow, jamming him in the bottom of the grave.

8

Soldiers

The small patrol of soldiers under Sergeant Biff Donovan rode across the creek a little way down-stream, shortly after noon. A few minutes later they found the dead men and the open grave.

'Jesus, Mary an' Joseph,' breathed Donovan, standing at the edge of the grave, looking down at the two sprawled bodies. 'There's enough blood here to paint the barrack room.'

'Another one over here, Sarge. He's been shot up to hell an' looks like he took some kinda fall.'

'Outa yonder tree, I reckon,' opined another soldier, pointing to broken branches and a piece of torn shirt that matched the one on Harve Gore's body.

Donovan lifted his hat and scratched at his thinning, sweaty hair. 'Well, that green lieutenant was right when he said he heard gunfire and it sounded like a fight. Only he was thinkin' of them Mescaleros we're tryin to find.'

'What we gonna do, Sarge?'

'Bury 'em. Dig the grave a bit deeper and put 'em all in together.'

The men groaned but knew it was the decent — the only — thing to do. 'What you reckon happened?'

Donovan had been studying the sign. 'One man agin two, I figure — and he was the better.'

'Which one?'

'Don't matter now, do it? Get 'em laid to rest, but check for identification first.'

Two soldiers straddled the shallow grave and grunted as they pulled Bill Redmond's bloody body off Benbow and heaved it aside. The younger soldier was sick, when he saw how torn up Redmond's chest was. The older man, easing Benbow into a position where he could grab him under the arms to heave out of the shallow grave, suddenly let out a cry.

'Hell almighty! This one's still alive!'

'After losin' all that blood?' scoffed the sergeant moving forward. 'You've got the jitters, Callaghan, so you have.'

'The blood ain't his, Sarge. It's from the fella who was lyin' across him. This one's got a chest wound just at his left armpit and the back of his head's had a wallop — it's kinda squishy.'

Sergeant Donovan examined the unconscious Benbow and sat back on his hams, tilting his hat down over his eyes now.

'Well, that damn shavetail loot is gonna want all kindsa reports writ up on this! Goddamn!' He poked Benbow roughly, the man's head rolling slightly. 'Why the hell couldn't you be dead, too, fella!'

'Aw, Sarge, don't talk like that!' complained the young soldier who had thrown up at sight of Redmond. 'That kinda talk's bad luck!'

'Is that so, Private Biddle? But it's *lucky* for this fella, whoever he is. Get the other two buried while the rest of us make a travois. Much as I hate the thought, we're gonna have to drag this one back to our spit-'n'-polish Loot. An' I bet he'll send him back to the fort to the sawbones.'

'Look on the bright side, Sarge. He might pick you to take him.'

Sergeant Donovan's answer to that was to spit copiously before he began shouting at his men to get moving.

'We dunno where them Mescalero renegades are. Mebbe they heard the shootin' too, an'll come to check up.'

That was incentive enough to get the soldiers hurrying about the chores they had been ordered to do.

★ ★ ★

Benbow groaned as he tried to move his head. It was thundering like a cattle stampede passing over his bed and . . . *bed!*

139

Groaning even louder he struggled to a half-sitting position and stared about him in the darkness. A lamp with the wick turned low was in one corner of a long, narrow room, throwing only enough light to intensify the deep shadows.

His vision was not entirely clear but he could make out the ends of four or five other iron-framed beds that matched the one where he lay. They were empty as far as he could tell. The strain on his chest was too great and he sagged back against pillows with a sigh, stifling another groan.

Some kind of infirmary, he decided. But how did he get here? Where was 'here' anyway . . . ?

He tried to move his left arm and found it was strapped to his chest, which seemed to be thickly bandaged. His head was crashing now, his vision shot through with spears of light that only served to confuse things.

He gave up trying to remember what had happened to him, having some vague idea of a gunfight — but that was all. He was still groping for memory when a wave of blackness overwhelmed him.

* ★ *

Then there was a man with a beet-red face surrounded by lots of greying hair bending over him. He smelled brandy and realized that waves of fumes were washing over him as the red-faced man breathed heavily and regularly.

'Ah, you've decided to join us at last,' the man said wearily. 'Pre-empting your question, you are in the infirmary of Fort Abel Landis on the Alamosa River, near Elephant Bluff. You were found lying in a shallow grave with two dead men, one lying atop you and — '

'I — recollect now — partly. You a — doctor?'

'I try to be. Name of Wilson, army rank of Captain, twenty-some years experience in patching up bullet wounds and removing poisoned arrowheads from various parts of men's — and, occasionally, women's — anatomy. In your case, it was a rifle slug that has ripped up your left armpit and damaged the tendons in your left arm, but nothing that won't heal in time.'

'How much — time, Doc?'

'And you have a touch of concussion where you apparently hit your head on a rock that was covered with a layer of dirt, judging by the amount I washed out of the wound. Time? You're a tough one, mister, I can see that. You bear the marks of previous wounds, the result of violence in some of its many forms. I'd give you another week or so.'

Despite the pain it caused him, Benbow shook his head. 'Too long, Doc! I've gotta get back to — my land. Prove-up time's fast approaching and — I-I have a lot to do yet.'

'One more week, mister,' Wilson said curtly. 'That's minimum. The colonel will wish to know who you are and what happened back there. He will no doubt have whatever story you tell him checked out. So, you will be our —

guest, until he's satisfied. I can assure you of that.'

Benbow swore softly, but admitted silently that he did not feel up to tackling the remaining chores on his cabin. Or even attempting the long ride back to his valley.

'It is somewhat intriguing: two dead men, both without identification, riding horses branded D-C, a well-known ranch south of here near Loma Vista. There is already a patrol in that general area after the Mescalero break-out, so a field telegraph message will soon have some answers for us. Although fairly seriously wounded, you seem to be the killer of the other men. So there is a chance you'll be here longer than the week I predicted.'

Damnit! He'd go crazy lying here!

'There's an armed sentry on the door, by the way,' the doctor added, as if reading Benbow's mind, gathering his tools of trade into a worn and scuffed leather bag stamped: US Army. 'We've had several attempted desertions by men who believed they could pull the wool over my eyes and make their escape by way of my infirmary.' He smiled thinly. 'None was successful.'

He nodded and made his way to the door at the far end of the room. He rapped some kind of signal and Benbow heard a key turn in a lock. The door swung open far enough for him to glimpse a man in uniform, holding a rifle with fixed bayonet.

*　*　*

Ivy Cartwright saw her father approaching through the street window. He was hurrying for a change and she felt the worry that had been eating at her these past few days knot her insides more intensely.

Please God, let him bring me some good news about Chance!

But Dave Cartwright's news was a mixture of good and bad. 'Benbow's alive and in the infirmary at Fort Abel Landis, Ivy.'

She put a hand to her mouth and hoped no customers would come in just now. 'What — what was he doing that far north?'

'Apparently tracking down Redmond and Gore. It appears he killed them both, but was wounded — not too seriously, it seems.'

She gripped the edge of the counter, feeling the blood drain from her face. Her father lit one of his cigars and she noticed his big hand shook a little. He leaned against the counter, his face, set in its usual hard lines, telling her nothing.

'I've had a gruelling interrogation by some damn jumped-up army lieutenant, demanding to know why I *sent* Benbow after Redmond and Gore. I told him he went of his own accord, and you know what he said: '*A bounty hunter like that don't need any urging . . .* ' Bounty hunter! I've often wondered where Benbow got his money to get started on that section of his up-valley — now I know.' His eyes glinted as they turned to her pale face. 'Now *you* know. And I'll not allow any daughter of mine to marry a *bounty hunter!*'

'He's not a bounty hunter, Dad,' she said quietly.

'Well, I expected you would say that, Ivy, but this lieutenant knows what he's talking about. He gave me times and places and it was all just before Benbow showed up here.'

'Dad, Chance has told me how he came by his money. It wasn't a bounty, as such.'

'Oh? There are different forms of blood money, are there? Some . . . acceptable? I think not, woman, and — '

'He was hired by a cattle association to find some stolen stock,' she broke in, jaw set firmly now, her eyes clear and steady. 'Chance trailed the men and there was a gunfight. He wounded both men and brought them in — and it turned out one was a wanted man in another county. There was a reward and it was paid to Chance. He didn't chase

146

any 'blood money' as you call it. It was a legitimate reward and he earned it.'

Cartwright frowned, smoked a few puffs and grunted. 'A fine line of distinction.'

'Oh, don't be so stubborn, Dad! Chance is a decent man and as I've told you a hundred times, I intend to marry him — with or without your permission.'

'Dammit, Ivy! I hope you don't have any loco ideas of going to see him at Fort Landis!'

She hesitated, shook her head slowly. 'No-oo. I did, but now I don't think I will, Dad. As long as he's recovering I'm content. But the deadline for his prove-up is drawing close. So, I'm going to hire Jimmy Tuttle's sister-in-law, Lucy Inglis, to run the store while I go out to the cabin and get it in as good order as I can in the time.'

'You're — what? May I remind you that this is *my* store and — '

'It's the family store, Dad. You

remind me of it, constantly, tell me what I'll be throwing up to become Chance Benbow's wife. I'm doing what I said. Lucy has helped out here often enough to know how to run it efficiently.'

'What d'you think you can do at the cabin? It hasn't even got all the doors and windows in. There's no furniture . . . '

'That's easily found — in your barn. We've tables and chairs, even beds there, just gathering dust under tarps, discarded. You could give them to me as a wedding present if you wanted. Or just plain give them to me.'

He was beginning to bluster, outraged, angry at her suggestions because he knew they would work out, and he realized that he hadn't got rid of Chance Benbow after all.

'Ah, do what you like! You're just like your mother!'

She leaned over the counter, brushed her lips across his leathery cheek, smiling.

'Thank you for the compliment, Dad.'

He strode out, muttering.

* * *

A week made a big difference.

Lucy Inglis's elder brother, Wilf, was 'resting' between jobs, but on his way to Santa Fe to join a big cattle company. At Lucy's suggestion, he spent a couple of days helping Ivy with the heavier work, rigged the chimney for the fireplace — which truly delighted Ivy, and brought in the old but still strong furniture from Cartwright's barn. They set it up inside, and Wilf swung the entrance doors and the remaining shutters on the windows.

She thanked him but he wouldn't accept any money.

'You been good to Lucy since she's been a widow, Ivy. This is my way of sayin' 'thanks' — in part, anyways.'

'Bless you, Wilf, and good luck with your new job in Santa Fe.'

She waved him on his way and looked around at the cabin. It was liveable enough, but outside: what remained? There were fences needed, which meant posts had to be cut and holes dug, wire rolls brought out from the store and strung. There would need to be a herd, too — she couldn't recall the minimum number of cattle required by the Land Agency, but she would somehow prevail upon her father to help out there. In fact, she might even talk him into lending her a man or two to help meet the deadline.

Alone the next day, she was sitting at the newly-scrubbed kitchen table, sewing some flowery material into curtains for the windows, when she heard a hail from the yard. Puzzled, Ivy hurried to a window, saw a rider out there on a big chestnut, leading a packhorse. He waved his hat and called,

''Morning, Ivy. You've got the place lookin' great. Heard you could use a hand while Chance's laid up. I've got time, muscles and money. Would I be welcome?'

She was too surprised at first to reply immediately and then she smiled, her dust-smeared face lighting up with pleasure. She hurried to the front door, automatically pushing her hair back into place.

'What a question, Wylie! Of course you're welcome! I'm so very glad to see you. Come on up!'

9

Homecoming

Eight days was as long as Benbow was prepared to stay at Fort Abel Landis. In fact, it was too damn long, really, but he heeded the doctor's advice about resting his arm and the wound at the edge of the chest and armpit.

'You go flapping that wing around like you're trying to fly, Mr Benbow, and you'll walk through the rest of your life — however long or short that may be — with your left arm no more than a stiff, useless stick. And your chest will hurt so constantly with every breath you take that you'll seriously consider amputation of that limb.'

Benbow looked at Doctor Wilson soberly. 'I figure you're exaggeratin', Doc, but mebbe not too much — just enough to scare me. And you've sure done that! OK, one week.'

'Ten days would be better.'

'Settle for eight?'

Wilson shook his head slowly but finally agreed. 'I believe you're tough enough, but you'll still need to go slow for a time. I suspect it's lucky it wasn't your gun arm.'

'I'm no gunfighter, Doc.'

'Tell that to the men buried in that shallow grave.'

'I can use a gun tolerably well,' Benbow admitted. 'I don't make a habit of it — only when I have to.'

Wilson stared steadily, then nodded once, curtly. 'I believe that, Mr Benbow.'

The eighth day dawned and when Doc Wilson entered the infirmary, the light still grey before actual sunrise, Benbow was dressed and waiting. His left arm was in a black sling and an edge of the firm bandages still around his chest showed at the open neck of his new denim shirt. Like the trousers and hat, it had been purchased at the fort's sutler's store.

'You're certainly not wasting any time!'

'Can't afford to, Doc.' Benbow thrust out his right hand and shook with the medic. Like most medical men, the handshake was loose and swift — delicate fingers could be bruised by over-enthusiastic hand-shakes. 'Thanks for all you've done.'

'I wish you well, Mr Benbow. I mean that.'

* * *

The doctor's words were still ringing in Benbow's ears when he made his first night camp amongst some rocks a long way from Fort Abel Landis — and a longer way still from his valley.

He was worried that he might not make the deadline now. Not only had he lost all that time chasing down Redmond and Gore, but there had been the long, boring days in the infirmary. But, he admitted silently to himself that he wasn't really fit yet. A long way from it.

He would need that left arm in top working condition and he rode holding an Army-issue can of beans. Doc Wilson had told him that the weight was just right for him to exercise the arm from the elbow — raise and lower, raise and lower — a hundred times a day as he rode. Also, the can was the right diameter for him to open and close his fingers around it, strengthening the hand. When he could, he was to raise the arm slowly above his head.

'It'll hurt like hell at first as the shortened tendons try to accomodate the stretching. You'll cuss and swear, most of it aimed at me, then yourself — and last of all at the man who shot you.'

Benbow did all those things, with savage enthusiasm. But the worst profanity, he was surprised to find, was aimed at himself, for getting into the situation that had caused the wound in the first place.

But that sobered him; no, no regrets. He had been obligated to kill the men who had murdered young Randy Kelso.

Now his obligations were to Ivy Cartwright — and also the Territorial Land Agency. For, if he did not make the prove-up deadline there would be no cabin or embryo ranch to take his new bride to.

Two days later, when he eventually topped out on the mountain that overlooked his valley where he had built the cabin, he felt his heart lurch and the world spin dizzily around him.

There was no cabin — only an untidy pile of blackened and charred timber, grass and brush, where the fire had swarmed down the slope.

And one other thing: a fresh grave on the slope that overlooked the bend of the creek.

He rode slowly down and, fearfully, read the headboard.

Here lies Ivy Cartwright . . .

He didn't read any more — *couldn't* read any more because of the tears suddenly welling into his trail-reddened eyes.

*　*　*

The town was called Saguaro and it straddled the New Mexico-Arizona line, just north of the San Francisco River.

It was writhing in the painted colours of a badlands sunset when the rider came in from the north-east, his big-chested dun trailing hoofs through the dust, head hanging, close to jaded.

The tall, stubbled man hunched in the saddle, almost as dusty as the weary horse, turned towards the livery where the hostler was lighting lamps for the darkness that was almost upon the town.

Without preamble, the rider spoke, still sitting the saddle, 'Take care of my horse — and I mean take care of him. You sluice him down with tepid water — not cold — and you give him fresh hay, not some mouldy grass. You curry-comb him, clean his hoofs, unstick all them burrs from his tail and mane — and if he don't look one hundred per cent better'n he does now, when I come back, you won't like the way I'll leave you lookin', neither.'

The livery man was about average build, but his arms showed knotted biceps because he wore a shirt that had had the sleeves torn off at the shoulders. He was about forty, a man used to horses and their wants, with a face that had been in close contact with a lot of fists over the years.

'I dunno who you are or who you *think* you are, mister, but you don't come in here threatenin' me in my own stables. No need for it. I can see your bronc needs attention and I'll give it to him gladly — and be happy to charge you plenty for it. You up to payin' in advance?'

'Long as you do all that I asked — and heed what I said'll happen to you if you don't.'

The man held out a callused, dirty

palm and the rider slapped a sawbuck into it. 'If there's more due, I'll pay when I come back.'

'Hey, this is way too much. I was only joshin' about overchargin' you . . . '

The man was already walking back through the big doors, carrying his dusty Winchester now, which he had slid from the saddle scabbard, with a left arm that seemed a mite stiff to the hostler. The man's right hand felt for the butt of his six-gun and eased it in the holster as he turned up the street. He walked slowly along, looking at the signs and false-fronts across the way.

He stepped down into the thinning evening traffic and several drivers of wagons and buckboards cursed him as they had to haul rein and fight their teams to allow him to pass. He didn't look around, ignored the curses, and stepped up on to the opposite board-walk. He pushed through the swing doors of a small diner called the Flapjack House.

Inside, people — mostly men, a few

with women — were eating at small tables scattered about. The man with the rifle drew their eyes and silence fell as he looked around, studying each male customer closely.

'I don't see Joe Harris.'

The customers stared. No one spoke.

He raised his voice. 'I'm looking for Joe Harris! I was told he eats here every sundown.'

A woman behind a small counter towards the back of the room, cleared her throat. 'That's right, mister. But you're a mite early. Joe don't usually come in till it's just on dark.'

The cold eyes looked through the open doorway at the shadows crawling across the street. 'I'll wait.'

He toed out a chair at a vacant table, sat down and laid his rifle in front of him, watching the door.

The woman cleared her throat again. 'Somethin' while you're waitin'? Coffee? Plate of flapjacks with fresh hive honey an' cream? Or bacon an' . . . ?'

The man didn't answer, his gaze was fixed on the doorway as two men came in talking, the shorter one chuckling at something the other said. The leading one looked as if he had been doing manual work; his shirt was blotched with dark patches of sweat, his face was gleaming with it. The short man dabbed at his eyes with a corner of his neckerchief.

'Joe, I dunno where you get them jokes, but you must have a couple hundred of 'em! An' each one's different!'

'Make 'em up as I go along,' said the first man with a touch of pride. 'I'm a real funny man when you get to know me.' He turned his head as the counter woman called,

'Fella to see you, Joe.' She gestured to the man with the rifle sitting at the table.

Joe Harris turned to look, frowned, tensing, when he saw the man stand, obviously in from long, hard trails.

'I remember you, Harris. You were

quite a ways downslope at Ensuelo Valley, but I recollect you.'

Harris was mighty wary now, still frowning. 'I know you?'

'Do you?'

'Listen, you look kinda familiar but — '

'It don't matter,' the man cut in. 'You're the first and I won't wait any longer.'

The way the man set himself, Harris knew he was going for his gun. Joe lunged for the startled shorter man, swung him in front of him with one hand while his other palmed up his Colt, shooting too soon, the lead splintering the floor a yard in front of the stranger.

The tall man's gun was out of leather and blasted two hammering shots, one taking the short man in the body and wrenching him from Harris's grip, exposing Joe. The second bullet knocked Joe halfway back across the room and he gagged, clawing at his midriff. Face contorted, he dropped to his knees as the customers scattered, women screaming, men cursing and stumbling to get out of the way.

The tall rider ignored them, walked forward with his six-gun still smoking, stepping over the short man who writhed on the floor. He stood above Harris who was looking up from a face barely recognizable in its twisted agony.

'What — who — ?'

'You know who — and why.'

The tall man shot him again and Joe was blown back another yard. This time he fell on his side, knees drawn up to his chest. He made no sound or movement now: he was already dead.

His killer looked down at him expressionlessly, reloading his Colt's cylinder by feel as he thumbed home fresh cartridges from his belt loops.

He lifted his rifle from the table and, without looking at Harris or the wounded man on the floor, went out into the new night. The last sunset colours were still fading from the western sky as he walked down to the livery and turned in through the big double doors.

* * *

He was sprawled on a pile of hay to one side of the hostler's office, coming awake slowly, aware of a harsh voice close by. Then a boot toe caressed his ribs. His eyelids flew up and his right hand appeared, holding his Colt.

'Don't do it, fella!' snapped the harsh voice and he saw the short man with the sawn-off shotgun standing at the entrance of the hay bay. There was a tin star pinned to his shirt, catching a little lamplight. 'I'd be in my rights to blast you after you just killin' Joe Harris and woundin' Shorty McRae.'

The killer sat up; he didn't holster his Colt, just kept it down beside his right thigh, thumb on the hammer spur. His left arm hung sort of stiffly, 'Harris fired first.'

'Because he saw you goin' for your gun accordin' to witnesses. They all

164

agree it was like a — an execution. Guess Shorty was lucky you only wounded him.'

'Didn't want him. Only Harris.'

'Why Joe? He wasn't a bad sort.'

'Says who? He rode with the Ryan gang.'

'Whoa! You're outa date, fella. Yeah, Joe used to ride with Moss Ryan's wild bunch, but he had a fallin' out about the time I nabbed him in a back room with a half-breed girl-child. He wanted a deal: if I'd go easy on him, he'd name the gang members, tell me where I could likely find 'em.'

'You fell for it?'

The sheriff's eyes narrowed. 'I don't 'fall' for things, I think 'em through. I weighed the pros and cons and the pros won. Harris was small change, anyway, the one they left to watch the getaway mounts, put out the camp-fires, cover their tracks.'

'That ain't such small change.'

'Was, compared to the rest of them killers. We did our deal, and I found

165

him a job diggin' rain channels round the town — that 'Frisco floods in a heavy dew, you know. He don't make a lotta money but he was happy enough — and knew I was there to protect him.'

Cold eyes stared the lawman down. 'Not always.'

'No. I was delayed out at a ranch this evenin' or Joe might still be alive.'

'Or you could be dead alongside him.'

The shotgun jerked a little and the tall man tensed.

'You got a high opinion of yourself, mister. I've seen quite a few posters of gunfighters but I don't recognize you. What name?'

The tall man hesitated. 'Chance Benbow.'

The sheriff frowned. 'Well, it's kinda familiar. Don't seem like I connect it with any killin' though! Wait! There was a cavalry loo-tenant passin' through here with a troop, lookin' for the last of them Apaches that busted out after the floods south of Socorro. Told some story about a fella, name of Benbow as I recollect, shot it out with two fellas who'd killed some friend of his near Loma Vista . . . You?'

The tall man nodded. 'Joe wasn't mixed up in that. He was part of the gang who murdered and raped the woman I was gonna marry, burned down my cabin and near-killed a damn good friend of mine named Wylie. *That's* why Joe Harris died. And the rest of Ryan's bunch'll die, too, before long.'

'Hold up, hold up! What the hell is this? You're goin' after Moss Ryan and his gang?'

Benbow looked at him bleakly, didn't speak.

'You claim they murdered your woman? Where was this?'

'Ensuelo Valley, north of Loma Vista.' Benbow's stubbled face seemed to set into even bleaker lines. 'Means 'Dreams'. We didn't name it, but it appealed to Ivy and me.'

'Ivy? You mean Ivy Cartwright? Big Dave Cartwright's daughter? Hell, I heard about that massacre a few weeks ago. Yeah! That's where I heard your name. Thought you'd been shot or somethin'.'

'I recovered. What're you aiming to do with me?'

The lawman seemed to think it over, the shotgun unwavering. 'When did this murder and rape happen?'

'Almost a month ago, couple of days before I arrived back in the valley.' There was solid bitterness in Benbow's tone and the small sheriff found himself feeling sorry for this tall, dangerous man who had come home to such awful tragedy.

'You got a date? No, I can work it out. Seventeenth? Eighteenth?'

'Wylie said the eighteenth.'

'Wylie? He was one got shot by the gang?'

Benbow nodded. 'He was helping Ivy get the place ready for prove-up for me while I was in an infirmary. They headshot him, also in the side. He fell unconscious and there was a lot of blood — they must've figured he was dead. When he came round the cabin was burning down around him and — and Ivy was . . .'

'That's all right, son, I get the idea.' The sheriff was no more than ten years older than Benbow but he spoke in a fatherly tone, affected by the big man's grief.

Benbow's bleak expression didn't change. 'Somehow he managed to drag her clear before passing out. When he came to, the cabin was just a pile of ashes and Dave Cartwright and his crew were there, having seen the smoke. Too damn late as usual to do anythin' useful.'

'I savvy your bitterness, Benbow.'

'I was even too late for her funeral.' Chance paused, swallowing. The sheriff let him have his brief, lonely seconds of silence. 'Wylie nearly died, but he pulled through and was well enough to tell me what had happened when I saw him.'

'Why would Ryan pick on your place?'

'Look, Sheriff, that part's a long story. Has to do with a Wells Fargo robbery and me shootin' a couple of Ryan's bunch. Guess this was some kinda payback.'

'My name's Athol Blair — '

'You were a Texas Ranger, weren't you?'

'Uh-huh.' He slapped his left leg. ''Til a Mex bullet took off most of my kneecap. I limp a lot but still shoot straight.' He jerked the shotgun. 'This is a fine equalizer. But never mind that. What I want to tell you, and you better b'lieve this, 'cause it's gospel: You killed the wrong man.'

'The hell I did! I been tracking down Harris for twenty-some days and nights and — '

'And if you'd bothered to check, you'd've found him on the eighteenth in the jail at Furnace Creek. He went there on business for me, but he got drunk, was in a fight over a woman.

Near killed some young fella who happened to be the only son of a big rancher thereabouts. Sheriff more or less had to throw Joe in jail. But he let him out early before the rancher could get some of his hardcases in to lynch Joe.'

'If he was out early, he could've gotten to my valley.'

'Mebbe. But think on this, Benbow: why would he join up with Ryan's gang again after he'd give up their names and hidin' places to me? Be a sure way to get killed himself, any fool can see that.'

Benbow thought briefly. 'How many of Ryan's bunch did you nab after Harris turned traitor?'

Blair looked slightly embarrassed. 'Only two. Brothers named Corbin. The other hideouts had been abandoned.'

'Old ones! Harris bought his way outa trouble with that half-breed kid, mighty cheap, Blair. He never told you nothin' worth while! He could still have joined up with Ryan again when they rode on my place.'

'Then why would he come back here?'

'Because you'd given him a good set-up here. He even had his own bodyguard . . . You!'

Athol Blair thought about it, yellow teeth chewing at one corner of his mouth. He suddenly shook his head. 'You're drawin' too long a bow, Benbow. I'm gonna have to look into this a lot deeper.'

'No.'

As he spoke the word, Benbow kicked Blair's maimed knee and the man yelled, the leg collapsed under him and he fell sprawling, dropping the shotgun. Benbow, still prone, drove a boot against the man's jaw, rose up and clubbed him on the back of his neck with his fist. The sheriff slumped unconscious.

The hostler appeared, sleepy-eyed, but swiftly taking in the situation as Benbow stood, holding his rifle. 'Hell, man — you are in *trouble*!'

'Saddle my horse for me.'

'Sure, but — but Athol takes his job real seriously. You're gonna have him on your neck before you've travelled a mile!'

Benbow gave the man a cold look.

'It'll take more than him to stop me doing what I have to.'

10

Trail of Dead Men

Clay Donner was lucky he lived so long.

If Benbow hadn't had to spend so much time shaking off Athol Blair and his posse, he would have died three days earlier than he did.

The hostler in Saguaro had been right: Blair was mighty put out by the way Benbow had jumped him in the livery stables. Chance figured Blair likely wasn't too worried about any bruises on his small body, though probably his kneecap was giving him more than a mild taste of hell after Benbow's kick. It would be the man's pride that had been hurt most and which was driving him to run Benbow down.

But Chance had his mission and not

Athol Blair, not hell, storm, flood, or even high water, would keep him from it.

He had been riding the frontier for twenty years and he knew it well. He had run traplines in the Alleghanys, the Rockies in Colorado and even the Sierra Madre. He had hunted bear and shot meat for the railroad camps. He had grubbed for gold and been buried for three days in a tunnel shaft collapse, dug his way out with his bare hands. He had tracked Indians, using their own tricks against them. Once or twice he had run with some wild boys — not quite wild enough to get their pictures on wanted dodgers — and he learned how to dodge posses. While doing this once, he came up with a mountain man who wore nothing but the skins of animals he killed, hardly spoke ten words in three months, yet taught him more about the wilderness in that time than he had learned in all the years before.

So he was able to shake Blair's posse,

though he didn't underestimate the old Ranger with the game leg. Blair had had a big reputation before that Mex bullet had forced him to resign and chase a sheriff's job in a jerkwater town like Saguaro.

He would want Benbow's scalp at all costs, likely would continue on his trail long after his posse disbanded.

But Chance lost the posse for good in a tangle of hills known as the Bunch of Grapes, west of Albuquerque. He used the moon and stars to find his way out, resting by day in hidden draws and caves. When he came out of the tangle of hills, he found he had to cross the Manzano Mountain range if he wanted to skirt the Pueblo reservation; the Pueblo Indians weren't warlike, but there were army patrols he didn't care to run into. Once past the reservation, he turned south and made a fast run down to Estancia, within a frog's leap of Laguna del Perro.

He had a full beard now and his big bay mount was mighty weary. Grub was low and water wasn't plentiful, though he figured he could locate some hidden Indian wells in a pinch.

When he saw Estancia — why the hell did they build so far from the lake and permanent water? — he wondered if it had been worth all the damn effort. It was a scattered town, the buildings mostly clapboard, though a few clustered together were adobe. That was likely the business section. God alone knew how folk made a living out here in this desolate-looking country; he had heard there were men who ran small cattle spreads back in the hills but had to pack in their water in horse-drawn, wheeled wooden tanks from the lake. Miles away!

'Well, if a hard life's what you want,' he said, still not understanding how anyone could live out here, bring a woman, raise a family . . .

He chopped off the thought like a blow from an axe severing some cord to that part of his brain. Thinking about families and folks' ordinary, everyday lives, was not allowed! Not by Chance Benbow — not since Ensuelo Valley . . .

He shied away from even allowing himself to think of the name. His guts churned. His chest seemed to crush in and clamp his heart. His brain throbbed and a searing pain burned behind his eyes. *Oh, Christ, Ivy . . .* !

All right! One thought and one only. The promise of a wonderful life had been within his grasp and then snatched from him. The only woman he had ever loved, ever would love, had died terribly. Now the only thing he lived for was to find the men responsible and kill them all. What happened to him, during or after, was never given consideration — just so he lived long enough to take his vengeance.

'To hell with anything beyond the last man I kill,' he said aloud, startling himself to a small degree. Then he clamped his cracked lips together and set the weary bay down the long, winding trail to Estancia.

The lake glittered and sheened like brilliant blue crystal, miles away. His tongue was swollen, his throat raw — but slaking his thirst could wait.

Till after he had killed Clay Donner.

* * *

The man was not where he had been told to look for him.

It was in the back room of a small cantina-like adobe building right at the south edge of town. He had been told Donner stayed there with a woman, occasionally made a fast trip with three or four other men, over the Manzanos to where the stageline angled through the foothills — and most times came back with bulging pockets.

It was perfect ambush country and Donner made a pretty good living on the proceeds. There was no law in Estancia; actually, there was a sheriff, but he made his way through life by looking at the world through the bottom of tequila and whiskey bottles.

What went on in his bailiwick was of no interest to him — as long as his liquor supply was kept up.

Donner and his friends saw that it was.

When Benbow arrived in the dim bar the few drinkers looked at him carefully but decided that, though he had a dangerous look, there was no smell of law about him. When he asked for Clay Donner there was a sudden air of wariness in the room and three men sidled out the rear door. The fourth one wasn't fast enough, not by a long shot.

Benbow stepped into his path, put a hand against the man's greasy chest and thrust him back against the wall.

'Where's Donner?'

The man was as big as Benbow and had had his mouth smashed in at sometime, likely by a big boot, though badly enough to consider the possibility that he had been kicked by a mule.

'Dunno no Donner,' the man said, his words so slurred Benbow had to concentrate to understand them.

'I think you're lyin', friend.'

The man's eyes blazed. 'An' I think I'm gonna kill you, you son of a bitch!'

The knife came out of nowhere and Benbow had to step back pronto as the blade glittered at his belly level. The point skidded off his brass bullet-belt buckle. He turned side on and lifted his left arm, bent it and drove his elbow into that snarling face. It hurt his arm — he hadn't used it so roughly since leaving Fort Landis — but it hurt the man with the smashed mouth more.

It mashed in his nose and he staggered, the knife momentarily forgotten. Benbow grabbed his hand and slammed the knuckles against the adobe. The man yelled and the knife fell with a clatter. The fat man behind the bar slid along with raised bungstarter but Benbow had his Colt in his right hand now, swung backwards and felt the jar as the gun slammed the fat man's head. He moaned and dropped out of sight. There were only two other men in the bar and they ran out the front entrance.

The man with the smashed mouth was down on his knees, trying to stop the flow of blood from his crushed nose. Benbow placed the gun muzzle between the staring eyes and thumbed back the hammer.

'This fella Donner you've never heard of — '

'Wait! Judas — wait up!' The words were slurred even worse in the man's terror and three times Benbow had to make him repeat what he was saying before he figured out Clay Donner was with his woman, but in a shack three rows back beside a slag heap from the days of the old silver-mines.

Benbow let the ailing man fall on his side at the foot of the wall and went out.

He found the shack easily enough, saw at once that at least one of the men who had fled the cantina had stopped by to warn Donner there was trouble coming. The woman was gone and there was a man with his shirt hanging out, trying to mount a saddleless horse which kept moving away from him. Benbow squinted: yes, that was Donner. He could recall the smooth-skinned face with the soft, womanish lips. Wylie had warned him not to be fooled by the helpless boyish look: Clay Donner was in his thirties and mean as a castrated cougar.

He saw Benbow and brought over the Colt he had been holding, his body screening it from Chance's view. He got off one shot and Chance dropped to one knee, shot the man's right leg out from under him. Donner grunted and fell and the horse shied away, running off. Donner tried to lift his gun, his face contorted in pain, but Benbow had time to stride forward and kick the Colt from his grip.

Then he kicked Donner in the face and stretched the man out. Clay clawed at his face with both hands, blood trickling between the fingers. Benbow reached down and twisted up a handful of the straw-coloured hair, yanking Donner's head back.

'Losing your pretty-boy looks fast, Donner. And you'll lose 'em a damn sight faster you don't tell me what I want to know.'

'Who — who the hell're you?'

Chance shook him roughly. 'Benbow! Don't try to tell me you don't recognize me.'

'I-I — dunno no Benbow!'

He cried out as Chance twisted one ear, pushed him back in the dirt and planted a boot on the man's chest.

'I-I can't breathe!'

'Long as you got enough breath to tell me where I'll find Ryan or Ben Silver — preferably both.'

Donner's eyes widened. 'I-I dunno! No, gospel! We had a — deal go bad. Moss said we'd do best to scatter . . . '

'The deal at Ensuelo Valley, you mean!'

Clay Donner frowned. 'I-I'm talkin' about Deadwood, man! I dunno no Consuelo Valley or whatever . . . '

Benbow hit him with the gun barrel, not hard enough to knock him unconscious but enough to draw blood from a split scalp. While Donner moaned and lay there dazed, Benbow unloaded his Colt, placed the gun in front of Donner's face, then pushed a single cartridge back into the cylinder.

He spun it quickly and when it stopped, cocked the hammer. Clay Donner drew in a sharp, deep breath as the muzzle was rammed against his temple.

He screamed and convulsed as the hammer fell — making a click of metal to metal that Benbow had no doubt sounded like an explosion inside Donner's head.

'Lucky that time, Donner. You got four more chances — or mebbe only three — or two — or — one. Mebbe none at all . . . '

He let the hammer drop again and Donner almost fainted as it clicked once more. Then he shuddered as he heard the hammer ratchet back to full cock.

'Three. Luck's gonna run out faster after this one — if you live past it.'

'Jesus, don't! Don't!' Clay was breathing like a locomotive at a water siding in desert heat. 'Oh, Christ, don't — *please!* I-I'll tell you where Ben Silver is. Honest to God I-I dunno where you'll find Ryan . . .'

'I'll settle for Silver. I'll find Ryan later. And McWilliams. None of you's gonna escape.'

11

Number Three

Clay Donner was treacherous to the last.

Before he died, he told Benbow where Ben Silver could be found — but neglected to mention that Ben was running with the Fayette brothers now, two of the roughest, toughest sons of bitches in New Mexico.

Or any other place.

The trail was long and thirsty and hungry, but Benbow was used to privation by now. He ate and drank because he had to to stay alive, and he had to stay alive at least long enough to take his revenge on Moss Ryan and all of Ivy's killers. It was becoming slightly easier to think about her now, for a few minutes at a time, anyway; to remember all the sweet and good things about her and the time they had shared. It always choked him up. He had never been an emotional man; his father had been too strict about that with the whole family back in Virginia. Were they still there? Building the tobacco empire his father had so desired? He'd never know now, because he would never get in touch with them again. But, maybe one day he would roll a cigarette and notice the *Benbow Fine Virginia Tobacco* label on the sack . . .

Silver had chosen mighty rough country to hide in. Benbow figured that the wild bunch had disbanded after the killing and fire in the valley, knowing the furore it would arouse. But though there were posses from Socorro, and Cartwright's hardcases, and the army patrols had been alerted, the killers had never been sighted.

The only way to find them all was Benbow's way.

He had never been vicious, nor had he killed gratuitously, but there had been a few other times in his life when killing had been necessary and he hadn't shied away from it. This time was different: it was eating into him like a cancer, destroying the man he once was — the man Ivy had been attracted to. That couldn't be helped: if he had to die to accomplish his mission, then he would — life only mattered now as long as he could find Ryan.

Silver would be number three — that would leave Ryan and McWilliams. The weather was growing colder now as he travelled north. But if he had to wade through a blizzard with snow up to his crotch, he would get the chore done. It had to be soon — the vengeance trail had been too long already.

Too many sundowns, where all he had to look forward to come daylight were more miles of badlands, lousy grub, not enough water. His clothes were beginning to hang on him and for a short time he hadn't even bothered bathing. Simply had no energy for it; he was burning up whatever he had in the hatred that swirled through his body twenty-four hours each day.

Eventually, sanity prevailed and he stopped at a small town he never did know the name of, bought some cheap Mexican-type, loose-fitting clothes in an Indian market, then spent time in the river out of town. He burned the old clothes and as the pungent smoke rose, he vowed that from here on he would take better care of himself.

He *had* to, otherwise his lack of care for his well-being might prematurely end his vengeance trail.

And that could never be allowed to happen.

Afterwards? Who the hell cared what happened afterwards? He sure didn't.

The trail took him into the Resurrection Hills up in Guadaloupe County, north of Fort Sumner. It was a damn long way from Ensuelo Valley and he wondered at Silver coming this far. He didn't know the man, though he likely had briefly seen him with Ryan's men when they had come to the valley that first time, bent on getting Wylie.

And how was Wylie doing? He felt a touch of guilt that he hadn't thought about his friend in a week. He had left him in the Loma Vista infirmary, recovering slowly from his wounds and burns. His burns weren't too bad, but he was lucky to be alive. He had suffered two gunshot wounds, one bullet creasing his scalp above the left eye. Blood gushed like a stuck hog's and this actually saved his life because the killers thought he was dead when he fell. The second shot had taken him in the side, angled upwards slightly, tearing across his lower ribcage, the bullet nicking his left arm as it passed on. If it had gone in instead of striking a rib and ricocheting, he *would* have been dead.

He had passed out, he said, but was vaguely aware of Ryan's bunch — and Ivy's screams. (Benbow stopped his thoughts here, had to let his breathing settle.) Then there had been silence, except for the heavy breathing of the killers. They had then smashed up the inside of the cabin and set it on fire.

'I dunno to this day how I managed to get out — an' take Ivy with me, Chance. I-I had to drag her, down on my hands and knees . . . I'm — sorry it was so — undignified . . .'

'The damn things you can think to be sorry about!' Benbow had replied, hardly knowing what he said, his mind in turmoil with Wylie's descriptions — or lack of them. There was just enough to spark Benbow's imagination. 'You've got nothin' to be sorry about, Wylie. You did damn good, considering.'

'It wasn't good enough.'

'No. But you did what you could and nearly killed yourself doing it. Tell me the names of every one of them. Give me detailed descriptions. Then I'll get going.'

Wylie, lying in the bed, bandages and plaster squares dotted over his arms and face, reached up a bandaged hand, touched his arm.

'Chance. You — dunno what you're

taking on. Ryan's bunch. Hell! You *know* what they're like. I don't have to tell you after what's happened. Just be careful — be *damn* careful.'

Benbow had told him he would be careful — careful to track down each one of them and kill them.

'And anyone else who gets in my way . . .'

Wylie hadn't liked that last bit. But he saw by the bleakness in Benbow's steely eyes that the man meant it.

He didn't give a damn about his own welfare or anyone else's — as long as he avenged Ivy.

* * *

The Fayette brothers were half-breeds from Canada — part French, part Crow or Blackfoot. They were handsome enough in a rugged way, but were quick to fight and usually used thin-blade, razor-edged knives at some stage, mostly at the end, carving their victim up with gut-wrenching brutality.

The man who told him Silver was now riding with them, an oldster who lived on the fringe of the owlhoot and had done for twenty years, tested the silver dollar Benbow gave him with a set of strong yellow teeth, nodded, and slipped it into his old buckskin shirt pocket.

'Friend, you watch them Frenchies. They fight with their feet a lot.'

'Their feet?'

'Yeah, jumpin' about, kickin' a man's privates into mush, stavin' in his ribs. Savvy-somethin' it's called. When they got their man all groggy and smashed up, the slim one, Pierre, reaches for his knife . . . ' He shook his head. 'I seen him go to work with it, slicin' and hackin'. They leave 'em to die slow, bleedin' like stuck pigs, an' it ain't pretty. T'other one, Pascal, he looks on and kinda — drools.'

Benbow grunted. 'You sure Ben Silver is runnin' with scum like that?'

'He is. Ben's done somethin' real bad, dunno what. But he figures with ornery bastards like them Frenchies to protect him . . . From what, I wonder? Mebbe someone like you?'

'Mebbe. Thanks, old-timer.'

The oldster had something to square with the Fayettes, Benbow was sure of that. The old fella followed him out to his horse, and as he mounted, called, 'If you got time, stop by and tell me how you killed them bastards.'

Benbow lifted a hand and rode on out, looking at the distant, smoky hills where he hoped to find Silver.

★　★　★

Men like the Fayettes operated on the fear they instilled in others by being so brutal and ruthless. Chance rode mighty warily, forcing himself to slow his pace. When he came to a bottleneck canyon and a shadow up on a ledge rolled down a boulder to block his retreat, he reckoned someone had gotten word to the Fayettes to expect him.

As soon as he heard the first crunching of the rock starting its fall and bouncing down to jam in the narrow entrance, Benbow dug in the spurs. The horse whinnied a protest at such treatment after carrying its rider so far and for so long, but obeyed the urging of the rowels. It leapt forward and then slewed sideways into the deep shadow of an overhang as Chance wrenched on the reins. He palmed up his six-gun and twisted in the saddle.

A man was half-exposed on the ledge, a carbine up to his shoudler. Benbow fired, triggered again, hard on the first shot. Dust spurted and the man reared back, his bullet ricocheting high above the now prancing horse. Crouching low, Benbow spurred around the corner of the overhang, hurried by two more shots. Out of sight, he quit leather in a leap, tumbling when he hit the ground. But he had his rifle now. He rolled in tight against the rockface as the gun above sought him with a ragged volley.

The shooter, whoever he was, was impatient, clambered over rocks on the ledge, trying to get a position where he could see Benbow more easily. Benbow waited and in a matter of moments the ambusher appeared, sliding down into a cranny that would give him protection and a good view of Benbow's position.

Chance's Winchester came up and he fired five shots as fast as he could work lever and trigger. He heard his bullets ricocheting from the broken walls of the rock cranny, saw dust spurting, glimpsed the man with the carbine covering his head with his arms. Then the man slumped and his gun tumbled out of the cranny, turning once before it hit the ground.

The gunfire filled the small canyon with slapping echoes, and they covered the small sounds of the second man, above Benbow, coming carefully down the overhang's side. He was almost above Benbow when his shadow gave him away and Chance spun on his back, wrenching the rifle around and up. The muzzle struck a protruding rock and although he fired, the shot was off target: the bullet tore a spurting line of dust to one side of the killer, spraying him with rock chips.

Sunlight glinted off a knife blade as he crashed down, almost on top of Benbow. Chance lost the rifle, the man's body knocking it from his grasp. A knee sank into his belly, an elbow struck the side of his jaw just under one ear and his senses spun as his head filled with a dullness that threatened to burst his eardrum. A swarthy, stubbled face appeared above him. White teeth bared and clawed fingers tried to gouge his eyeballs from their sockets. He felt a searing hot pain across the top of his shoulder and knew the blade had missed the big artery there by a whisker. He didn't give the killer a second chance.

He rolled violently, upsetting the other's balance briefly, arched his back, hooked with his left fist. The blow lacked power because of his weak arm but it stung the Frenchman's large nose and blood showed at the cavernous nostrils. The man snapped his head forward but Benbow got his left hand up in time to divert it. Then he brought his right hand over, and slammed his Colt hard against the 'breed's head.

Fayette grunted and tumbled to one side. Benbow scrambled to get out from under, then the other spun and a boot caught him alongside the head, withdrew slightly and came back, snapping with the power of a horse's kick. He thought his head was being torn from his shoulders and he went away from the world for a short time into a grey place where everything was out of focus and filled with a roaring sound.

When he came back, he saw a man in dusty clothes, the left sleeve almost torn off his shirt at the shoulder, squatting, looking at him over the top of a bloody kerchief which he was holding to the lower half of his face.

His other hand held a flat blade with a handle wrapped in rawhide thong. He lifted the knife slightly.

'Note it well, *mon ami*,' he said, voice muffled by the kerchief. 'Here is the instrument of your death.'

Benbow said nothing, looking for his guns. The rifle lay in the dust where it had fallen, a couple of yards away. The six-gun was nowhere in sight.

'You 'ave killed my brother — now I must kill you. I 'ave almost decided how many cuts I will make before I allow you to die. I think — I think I will settle for — seventy-two. Does that number appeal to you, *m'sieur?*'

'I'm not interested in you, *mon-sooer*. All I want is Ben Silver.'

The Frenchie smiled thinly. 'Ah! Sil-ver! *Merde*! He bring you to us, to our good hideout. The *fou vengeur* — the crazy avenger who comes for him. You are *très dangereux* — very dangerous, it seems — but — ' He shrugged, made an expressive motion with his knife. 'Look now, eh?'

'You kick too damn hard, mister.' Benbow grimaced as he rubbed the outside of his lower right leg. 'They warned me you fight with your feet.'

'*Oui. La Savate. Bon, eh?* Good?'

Benbow nodded slowly, still rubbing his leg. 'Good. But not good enough.'

The 'breed's eyes arched. '*Non?* Why you think that?'

'This is better.'

Benbow's hand came away from his leg near his boot top with a derringer that blasted even as the 'breed's arm went back at astonishing speed, preparing for the knife throw. But the bullet was faster and smashed his nose flat before he could release the knife. He crashed backward and fell on to his side, legs moving jerkily, before becoming still.

Chance looked at the small, smoking gun: he had bought a matching pair of them from a drummer, giving one to Ivy after a drunk had tried to molest her in the store. Now he pushed it back into the top of his boot, breathing hard.

He had been hurt and moved stiffly, rubbing his left arm, especially up near the shoulder where he was bleeding. But it was only superficial and he stuffed a kerchief over the wound, under his shirt, picked up his rifle and found his six gun where it had been thrown against the rock. He checked the man who had rolled down the boulder, obviously the other French Canadian. He was dead, like his brother.

So — where was Ben Silver?

While searching for a way out of the canyon, he found the outlaw. The raucousness of crows led Benbow to the body. It was lying on a patch of stubble grass some yards beyond a still water hole in a sandstone hollow.

Silver had bled tremendously, the grass and parched earth beneath him were red and sodden. Benbow lost count of the cuts on the body after forty-six. The crows had also been at work; Benbow figured the Fayette brothers were no loss to the human race.

He was turning away, looking for a

bush he could cut a stake from so as to dig a grave for Silver, when the man startled him by moaning.

Squatting, he shooed the persistent crows away and gave Silver some water from his canteen. It spilled out of his slack mouth because the Fayettes' blades had done their butchery on his lips. 'You know me, Silver?'

The man nodded. 'S-sh-shoot me!' he pleaded weakly.

The man's lower body had been mutilated and Benbow swallowed his gorge, splashed a little more water on the bloody face. 'Moss Ryan. I have to find him.'

'Sh-shoot me — please!'

'Tell me where to find Ryan. Then I'll end your misery, Ben.'

Silver was silent except for his rattling breathing. He was gathering strength to speak, started to raise his head but the effort was too much. 'R-Rose . . .'

'Rose? You mean Santa Rosa?'

The head rolled — paused — rolled

back. 'P-Pecos — River. San — San . . .'

He convulsed and let out a shriek that brought goosebumps to Benbow's skin. Then the man slumped and Chance stood slowly, thumbing back his hat.

'Guess I just saved a bullet,' he said quietly.

12

Hang 'N' Rattle

The town of Santa Rosa was on the Pecos River, three days' ride from the canyon where Ben Silver had died with the Fayette brothers.

It was a large town by the usual standards in this part of the country. The sheriff was one Jake Manton, an experienced lawman with a tough reputation. He never played favourites, never persecuted — try bribing him and you'd find yourself looking at the world through a set of iron bars in Manton's cell block.

He was barely into his thirties and folk were often surprised that a man that young could have earned such a reputation. It sat easily upon his broad shoulders. He was a fearless man, had faced down drunken cowhands, loco gunfighters who figured he couldn't be as tough as men claimed. He had fought men to a standstill with his fists, men bigger than he was, once three at a time. And dragged them all off to jail.

So only a blamed fool would come to Jake Manton's town and hope to rob the bank and get away with it.

Moss Ryan said to hell with Manton: he was flat broke and had it on good authority that the Santa Rosa bank was sitting on a payroll for the Pecos Silverado Mining Company to the tune of almost 12,000 dollars.

'If I can't get me a fistful of that, I don't deserve to live!' Ryan claimed in the shabby, liquor-reeking back-country trailside bar in the hills west of Santa Rosa.

'It's temptin', all right, Moss,' agreed one of the trail-dirty group he was drinking with. 'But it can stay there for me, every damn cent of it, long as Jake Manton's packin' a star — an' his gun.'

The other four or five drinkers murmured agreement. Ryan, not as drunk as the others, but burning with the need for a decent getaway stake, scowled.

'Bunch of old women! Ought to've knowed better'n to come here and try to get you to share with me. What we got here? Six, countin' me. That's three thousand for me, nine thousand to divvy-up between you five.'

'That don't work out even-Steven!' complained a man with a horselike face and a runny nose which kept his long upper lip constantly damp.

'Sure it does,' Ryan told him in a dangerous voice. 'I thought this up. I get the extra thousand.'

'Who the hell you think you are?' snapped the man with the horse face. 'You might be a big-head down around Socorro, but you're no one up here, Ryan. Just a name with nothin' to back it up.'

Ryan's six-gun came up blasting and the horse-faced man was smashed back past the end of the rickety bar and into the clapboard wall. He struck with enough force to splinter the plank before he fell to the earthen floor, his big mouth open and gasping, but not for long. Every man there heard his death rattle.

'You figure that's enough back-up?' Ryan demanded.

In another fifteen minutes he had three men agreeing to join him. The fourth man slipped away while they were toasting each other and the success of the coming bank raid.

'That young ranny better keep his damn mouth shut,' growled Ryan, meaning the one who had run off.

'Aw, Cappy's OK. Got himself a young wife. He's kinda scared about takin' risks, that's all.'

Ryan grunted. 'All right. Well, let's get down to details . . . '

But Cappy was not 'all right'.

He had a young wife, as the man had told Ryan, and he had just learned she was pregnant. She was tearful, too, crying about the kind of lawless life Cappy led.

'How we gonna manage, Cap?' she sobbed. 'How can we bring a baby into this kinda life? We got no money. I need a decent doctor, too, bein' narrow in the hips the way I am — and somewhere nice to come home to. Not this dump. Some place where we can give our baby a chance, like we never had ourselves, neither of us.'

Cappy knew she was right but he had been angry with her and stomped off to bed. Lying awake, and with a streak of decency in him he hadn't been aware of, he decided he had to do something about getting some money — and moving into a good town like Santa Rosa, instead of hiding away back here in the hills. At first he had been tempted to join Ryan, but knew no matter what the seasoned outlaw said, it would be mighty dangerous trying to rob a bank in Jake Manton's town.

Then it had come to him: he could go to Manton and lay it on the line for him; he would tell what he knew about the robbery in exchange for a reward, a doctor to care for his woman and the chance of a life as a normal citizen.

Everyone knew Manton was tough, but Cappy had heard the sheriff had a humane streak in him, too, would give a man a break if he was convinced he meant to live a law-abiding life.

So he kissed the tear-wet face of his young wife, mounted up, and, in the night, rode down out of the hills, approaching the sheriff's office by way of the weed-grown lot behind the law building.

★   ★   ★

Moss Ryan became too involved in his plans for the robbery to worry much about Cappy, dismissing him as gutless.

Bad mistake.

For, while the actual robbery went off without a hitch, the getaway was a disaster. In fact, there was no getaway worthy of the name.

Jake Manton was waiting when the four robbers burst out of the bank, the sacks of money in their hands, ready to run down the alley to where they had left their fast mounts.

'Reckon you might need a hand totin' all that money, Ryan,' Manton called from behind a wagon that had been run into place while the outlaws were in the bank.

Six deputies stepped into view from various strategic places on the board-walks and the street. Cappy was one of them. Jake agreed to pay him a reward, but only if he helped stop the robbery. 'Earn your blood money,' he had told him.

Ryan saw Cappy and swore, letting his panicked confederates run past him. They started shooting and the rifles and a sawn-off shotgun from the lawmen cut them down in their tracks, scream-ing, bodies rolling, one sack bursting open and spilling a glitter of coins into the gutter.

Ryan jumped back inside the bank, spun in time to see the manager staggering out of his office, face streaked with blood from the gunwhipping he had taken, fumbling at a six-gun in shaking hands. Ryan bared his teeth, savagely angry, fired twice, his lead bringing down the grey-haired banker. One of the female clerks screamed and Ryan spun, shooting again without hesitation or thought — wild with rising panic and the knowledge that within minutes he could be dead — all because of that soppy goddamn kid, Cappy!

He grabbed the screaming woman by the arm and she almost collapsed when he thrust the hot muzzle of his Colt against her neck. 'Faint and I'll kill you, you bitch!' Ryan snapped, dragging her stumbling towards the street door.

Manton and his men were running forward and Ryan fired, bringing down the sheriff, who rolled in the dust, not fatally hit, but his shotgun had skidded out of reach.

'Get me a hoss, Cappy!' Ryan yelled. 'Get it or I blow her head off! An' you'll be responsible!'

He twisted the gun into the soft white neck of the woman and she cried out, sobbing.

Lying in the dust, holding a blood-spurting thigh, Jake Manton gritted: 'Do like he says! No one try to stop him! The money ain't worth Miss Merrilee's life!'

Cappy, heart thumping, ran down the alley and grabbed a fast-looking sorrel. He dragged it back to the front of the bank. Using the woman as a shield, Ryan mounted awkwardly, then hauled her up behind him, snapping,

'Put your arms around me, dammit! And hang on!'

She obeyed, terrified. Then Ryan shot Cappy down in cold blood.

'Double-crossin' son of a bitch!' he yelled and spurred the sorrel away down the street.

No one fired in case they hit the sobbing woman bank teller who was clinging desperately to Ryan.

★ ★ ★

213

Chance Benbow was slaking his tremendous thirst with a cold beer in the bar of a large saloon on the north side of Santa Rosa's plaza two days later. The room was crowded, the drinkers animated. He tried to sort out from all the shouting and catcalling what the excitement was about.

It didn't take him long to figure it out: there was going to be a hanging, the first in the town for five years. There was a special gallows being built out along the river. He had noticed some activity out that way but had entered the square at an angle and the buildings had prevented him from seeing clearly what was being constructed. He was signalling the barkeep for another beer when someone placed a hand on his arm.

He turned and looked into the sober face of Sheriff Manton. Surprised some, Benbow nodded. 'Howdy, Sheriff.'

'Howdy yourself. You're still wearin' your gun, fella.' The lawman leaned on a walking-stick, his face unsmiling.

That was what was different about this crowd! Chance sensed something but only now registered that everyone was unarmed.

'I've just arrived in town. Am I breaking some local law?'

'You are, till after the hangin', which is tomorrow.' Manton told him. 'There're notices all over town. Can't you read?'

'Yes. But I never saw any notices. Leastways, any I wanted to read. Had too big a thirst.'

'Kill it then, but don't get drunk and cause trouble. Meantime, hand over your gunrig to that man.'

He gestured with his stick to a smoky corner of the busy barroom, where Benbow could just make out a man with a deputy's star sitting at a long wooden table that held a dozen or so gunrigs and bullet belts.

'You can pick it up on your way outta town.'

Manton stood by while Benbow

complied with his order. He watched the trail-stained stranger pocket the receipt. 'You come in just to see the hangin'?'

'Never knew one was on — and it ain't my idea of entertainment. Picked up on the fact it's the first in five years. Must've been some crime.'

Manton looked a little tight around the mouth. 'Biggest since I been sheriff — and the last if I have any say in it.' He saw that Benbow was still curious and hadn't been going to explain, but he found himself adding, 'Bank robbery. Lot of folk killed. We nailed 'em all in the street except the ringleader. Got him later. That son of a bitch took a woman teller hostage then shot her along the trail. He stopped off at a cabin in the hills and murdered a young woman there, wife of a fella he reckons sold him out.'

'Miserable sonuver! I'm looking for a fella you might have a dodger on. Name of Moss Ryan.'

Jake Manton stiffened. 'Why you

lookin' for him?'

Benbow met the hard stare with one equally cold and unwavering. 'I aim to kill him. He murdered the woman I was gonna marry and . . . ' He stopped at something in the lawman's face. His belly suddenly tightened. 'You know him!'

Manton nodded gently. 'And I aim to hang him tomorrow mornin' at nine o'clock.'

* * *

It had taken some doing, but eventually, after hearing Benbow's story, the sheriff agreed that he could see Ryan in his cell.

'You wouldn't've killed him in my town and walked away from it, Benbow. I have to tell you that.'

'Well, I'll be happy to see the snake hang 'n' rattle as they say in Texas.' He lifted his arms as Manton patted him down, took his clasp knife and found the little derringer in his boot top.

The sheriff's gaze snapped. 'You think you were gonna shoot him in his cell with this?'

Benbow shook his head. 'No, it's just my back-up.'

'You get it when you leave town — right after the hangin'. I don't like vigilantes, Benbow.'

'Like I said, I'll be happy to see the bastard swing.'

'That he will.' Manton hefted the derringer, shook his head. 'Some back-up. I seen a fella get hit in the head and the belly with one of these and he still killed the man who shot him. One of my best deputies at the time . . .'

Manton waited down the passage as Benbow peered through the bars. Ryan was stretched out on the narrow bunk. He looked around incuriously, then swung his legs over the side when he recognizd Benbow.

'Judas priest, I heard you were comin'. How the hell you track me down?'

218

'I had some help from your old gang. They're all dead now, Ryan.'

Moss looked pale and gaunt, knowing he had only hours to live. His hands whitened around the bars. 'I — reckon I'd've preferred a bullet from you than that damn rope that's waitin' for me.'

'You might've got a bullet in the end — but you'd've been begging me to give it to you.'

Ryan frowned. 'The hell you got it in for me so much? I never did nothin' to you. That damn Wells Fargo posse saw to that. I just wanted Wylie because he knew where the strongbox was hid.'

Manton hurried, limping, as Benbow suddenly drove a fist between the bars into Ryan's face. The blow knocked him back into the middle of the cell, blood spurting as he swayed. The sheriff shoved Benbow against the wall with his stick. 'That's it! Get outa here!'

'I need to know where the last man's hidin' out! Fella named Troy McWilliams.'

Ryan looked up, blood dripping from

his chin. 'Troy? Hell, I ain't seen him since Deadwood. I dunno where he is. Wouldn't tell you if I did.'

'Liar! He was with you when you burned my cabin and murdered Ivy!'

Ryan frowned. 'What the hell you talkin' about? We never touched your damn cabin. And I dunno no 'Ivy'.'

'You scum! You just left Wylie for dead and then — turned on her!'

Manton dragged Benbow down the passage now, awkwardly, because of his cane, drew his gun and threatened the man with it.

'Come on! You're one damn pain, mister! You leave him be. No matter what he denies or admits, it won't make no difference come nine o'clock tomorrow morning.'

★ ★ ★

Benbow spent a restless night, didn't eat breakfast, and was in the front row when they dropped the trap out from underneath Moss Ryan. He stood there

220

with the suddenly silent crowd until the last twitch and shudder had passed through Ryan's dangling body . . .

Then he went looking for Troy McWilliams, the last of the killers. It took a week but he found him.

McWilliams died in his mountain cabin where he had been hiding out, but Benbow felt little satisfaction.

With his last breath, McWilliams — like Ryan, Silver, Donner and Joe Harris — had denied burning his cabin or murdering Ivy Cartwright. *All had denied it!*

Suddenly, he felt a painful knot in his belly.

God almighty! Could he have hunted down and killed the wrong men . . . ?

13

The Last Sundown

Doctor Sharpe was as busy as a family of squirrels hoarding nuts for the coming winter. He was red-eyed and irritable from lack of sleep as he moved from one man to the other of the small, sad, battered group in his infirmary. They all required attention in some way for bruises and cuts, or worse, one or two simply for a terrible hangover.

He glanced briefly over his shoulder as a weary Benbow followed him about.

'Would you believe that two trail herds hit our town last night?' The doctor shook his bald head, wonderingly. 'Months since we've seen more than a dozen cows in one bunch then two herds come in — from different directions, but both heading north to the railroad. And, naturally, there had to be challenges and disagreements over women, and . . . Well, just look at this sorry bunch! The saloon's a shambles and — '

'Doc, I can see it's been tough for you,' interrupted Benbow. 'And you're doin' a good job — but I want to know about Wylie. Is he OK? Where can I find him?'

Sharpe frowned. 'He's been gone for over a week. I don't know where he is.' He paused. 'He did say something about going to work on his . . . gun arm. He wanted to be able to help you — if you needed him.'

Benbow nodded: sounded like Wylie. 'He's OK then?'

'Yes. Good recovery. Very lucky. If those had been the usual heavy-calibre bullets he'd have been a dead man.'

Benbow was turning away but now spun back. 'What's that mean, Doc?'

Sharpe sighed, paused while bandaging a sick-looking trail hand's broken nose. 'Just what I said. He was lucky he was shot with a small-calibre gun.'

'I thought he was pretty bad when I saw him.'

'Oh, yes, shock can do that to a man. He knew how close he'd come to dying and often such a realization hits harder than the bullet.'

Benbow was reluctant to go, and just as reluctant to ask his next question, but he needed the answer.

'Any idea what calibre he was shot with, Doc?'

Sharpe gave him an exasperated look. 'Benbow, I'm very busy. I don't know what calibre.'

'You dug the lead out of his arm, didn't you?'

'Ye-es — well, I'd have to guess. Maybe a .32 or possibly .36; certainly no larger. I don't know what your interest is, Benbow, but if you are quite finished . . . ?'

Benbow lifted a hand in a salute of 'thanks' and left.

His money was very low now so he saved a few cents by passing up the bath house and washing in the river under the small wooden bridge. His shirt fell apart, split clear up the back and the collar was already adrift. He rolled it up and tossed it into some weeds and, in his worn undershirt, feeling the bite of the rising wind that heralded winter, he went down to the store.

He felt his heart skip a beat and then begin to race. There was a woman behind the counter and just for a moment he thought . . . But it couldn't be Ivy. It was Jim Tuttle's sister-in-law, the widow, Lucy Inglis, who had hair the same colour as Ivy's, and an abundance of it like her.

The store closed in around him, the position of every item, every smell reminded him of her and the times they had had quiet conversations over the scarred counter between customers . . .

'Oh, my! Chance! I hardly recognized you.'

He gave the widow a faint smile. ''Scuse my appearance, Lucy. I need a shirt. Blue if you have one.'

He fiddled while she searched the shelves, then she came back with a shirt, saying, 'I'm a pretty good judge of sizes. I think this'll fit.'

He was buttoning it up when Big Dave Cartwright came in through a door that led to the rear of the store, some invoice papers in his hand. He stopped when he saw Benbow.

'Thought I knew the voice. It's much the same, but you sure look . . . different.'

'Howdy, Dave. Yeah, I'm different.'

'You — accomplished your mission?'

Trail-red eyes looked at him coolly, the voice was tight. 'Killed five men. Men who deserved to die, I guess.'

Cartwright frowned. 'Ryan and his scum?' Benbow nodded. 'Well, it won't bring Ivy back . . . ' The rancher's voice faltered a little at her name, 'but there is some satisfaction knowing her killers have paid the price.'

Benbow said nothing, asked the Widow Inglis, folding cloth a few feet away, how much he owed and began to count out some change.

'Dammit, forget the money,' Cartwright snapped. 'Take the shirt and anything else you need.'

'All I need is to find Wylie.'

Cartwright frowned. 'Wylie? Why, he's camped up on Signal Knoll. Using my old line shack up there. I've told him he's welcome to stay as long as he likes. He didn't save Ivy, but he gave it a damn good try.' He saw Benbow's bleak face, mistook the reason for it and added quickly, 'As I know you would've if you'd been here, Benbow.'

'You've softened some.'

The rancher looked uneasy. 'I'm just realizing the . . . all those years I wasted, fighting with Ivy . . . ' His voice was a mere whisper. 'Now . . . '

Benbow felt a flash of pity for the older man who, like most folk after the loss of a loved one, realized too late that the type of relationship he had wanted with Ivy, but had been too stubborn or proud to admit, could never be now.

'We all miss our best chances some time, Dave. I might take you up on a sack of grub before I head out for Signal Knoll.'

Dave nodded. 'What will you do now?'

Benbow shrugged.

'Why do I get the feeling you don't want to tell me?'

'Mebbe I don't know — yet.'

Cartwright turned to the widow and told her to fix a grub sack for Benbow and throw in a carton of ammunition. When she went into the back room to do this, he said,

'You — wouldn't care to stay in the valley?'

Benbow's head came up sharply. 'Nothing for me here. Cabin's gone, *land*'s gone, seeing as I didn't prove-up — and Ivy's gone.'

'There's Ivy's . . . resting place.'

'I'll visit from time to time, I guess.' Benbow's voice was hoarse, his words curt.

'I . . . bought that land outright when

228

it came on the market after you'd missed prove-up. Because she . . . Ivy wanted it so bad. I've had a marble headstone made and a permanent rock border around the grave. It's more like a . . . shrine now.' He paused, looked steadily at Benbow and added, 'I've never found a really good replacement for Bill Redmond, but if you need a job . . .'

Benbow knew that Cartwright was trying to salve his conscience over the way he had acted; this was his attempt at smoothing over his own turmoil and grief. Chance was about to tell him he wanted no charity from him, then paused; Ivy had always wanted to see friendship between Chance and her father. Maybe she knew it could never really be that, but she would have settled for a kind of . . . truce.

'I've something else to do, Dave.'

'Well, can I help? I've got thirty men working for me and if any one of them can lend you a hand . . . ?'

'No. I have to do this myself.'

'Well, think about my offer.' Cartwright was trying hard but he couldn't quite keep the 'take-it-or-leave-it' edge off his words. 'I . . . meant it.'

Benbow lifted the sack the widow brought back. 'Thanks for this, Dave. *Adios* for now.'

Cartwright frowned after him, mouth tightening.

'He's a very troubled man still, Mr Cartwright,' the Widow Inglis said quietly. 'And still grieving very strongly for Ivy.'

'So am I! Now I've got some queries on these here invoices if you can spare me a few minutes.'

★ ★ ★

He heard the gunfire long before his horse zigzagged its way up Signal Knoll.

Single shots, spaced pretty much evenly, then rapid fire, followed by random shots.

'Using targets,' he murmured. 'Six-gun, not the rifle.'

He rode through some trees, noting the rays of the sun were slanted sharply as it dropped slowly in yet another sundown. Maybe, after all this time, the last one . . . ? He came to the clearing around the weathered line shack. Wylie was standing in the shade of a small shed where tools and working gear were dumped after use. He was facing a string of cardboard targets nailed to a post that was splintered at the edges and sagged a little.

There was also a man-sized wooden cut-out, peppered with bullet holes — mostly at the chest and around waist level. But several had splintered the head section, too.

'Pretty damn good,' Benbow announced as he halted his roan at the edge of the timber.

Wylie spun and dropped flat. His six-gun jumped as he triggered two rapid shots.

Benbow dived to one side, having felt the air-whip of a bullet past his face. He drew his Colt in mid-air and hit the ground, rolling, the horse snorting as it pranced out of the way.

Flopping on to his belly, elbow rammed into the ground, hammer spur under his thumb, trigger depressed, he dropped the pistol's barrel in line with Wylie.

'Jesus, Chance! You startled the hell outa me!'

'I startled you! You damn near blew my head off.'

'Hell, I'm sorry. I-I was concentratin', trying to call up an image of Moss Ryan, and then your voice. Christ, Chance, I'd never've forgiven myself if I-I'd . . .'

Benbow was on his feet now — neither man had holstered his gun — facing the other. 'You're faster — and those targets have had the hell shot out of 'em.'

'Yeah. I know it looks like I'm gettin' ready for a war — but . . . Why the hell didn't you send me word? I've been thinkin' Ryan or one of his other scum must've backshot you, or ganged up and bushwhacked you! I was gonna come lookin'.'

'Been kind of busy, Wylie. Travelled a helluva lot of miles tracking 'em down.'

'But you . . . got 'em all?'

'They're all dead. I killed Donner and Harris and McWilliams.'

Wiley seemed tense. 'What about Ryan? And Ben Silver?'

'Ben'd started running with the Fayette brothers. When they heard I was coming after him they sliced him up, didn't want to tangle with me.'

'You tangled with the Fayettes?'

Benbow nodded, left it at that. 'As for Ryan, he botched a bank hold-up in Santa Rosa, killed a female teller and the wife of a fella he reckoned had double-crossed him. Damn' fool, tryin' that in Jake Manton's town. I stayed for his hangin'.'

Wylie stared for a long moment, then smiled crookedly, lowered his Colt's hammer and rammed the gun back into the holster. He let his hand rest casually on the butt.

'Moss used to say he was born to be hung — but he hated the thought of it.'

'He went out well enough. Cussing the hell outa Jake Manton — and me.'

'Oh? You tangle with him before he stretched rope?'

'Not so much 'tangled'. But he blamed me for getting him hung — said if I hadn't been after him, he wouldn't've tried to hit that bank for a getaway stake. You know how these fellas are: it's always someone else's fault.'

Wylie chuckled. 'That'd be Ryan! Never put a foot wrong, always bein' hounded for somethin' he never done.'

'Funny you should say that, Link. He claimed he hadn't been near Ensuelo Valley or my cabin, since that day the Fargo posse set him a' running. Said he'd never set eyes on Ivy.'

'Well, hell, he would say that, wouldn't he?'

'Mmmm, mebbe. He was gonna hang no matter what. No point in denying the other things . . .'

Wylie's frown deepened. The only sounds were those of the insects coming to life now that the sun was going down, the occasional stamp of the roan's feet, a tinkle of harness buckles.

'What're you trying to say, Chance?' Wylie sounded very puzzled, ran a tongue around his lips.

'Well, strange thing is, every one of Ryan's men Joe Harris, Ben Silver, McWilliams, Clay Donner — they all claimed they hadn't been near the valley since the Wells Fargo posse drove 'em off. They went all the way up to Deadwood but run into so much trouble, the gang scattered — never joined up again.'

Wylie scoffed, moving his weight from one foot to the other now. 'That's eyewash, Chance! They damn near killed me when they rode in and caught me flat-footed at the cabin, helpin' Ivy with the new pantry door. Then they . . . Hell, I don't want to go over all that again, Chance. But they lied to you. It don't surprise me any.'

'Nor me at first. Till I got to thinkin' why *all* of 'em denied it. And Doc Sharpe told me you were wounded by small-calibre slugs. Like those fired by Ivy's derringer that I'd bought her to keep in her apron pocket for drunks who bothered her in the store. You saw it a couple of times.'

Wylie was mighty tense now. 'Lemme get this straight. Are you sayin' . . . ? Hell, 'course you're not! You know damn well I'd never do anythin' to hurt Ivy!'

'Mebbe you didn't mean to. You liked her a lot, Link, I know that. She told me a few times she was uneasy the way you looked at her, a couple of off-colour things you'd said when there was just the two of you.'

'Wh-aat!' Wylie half-laughed. 'You're not serious!'

'I figure you rode in, when I was off after Redmond and Gore, and somehow got carried away, tried to force yourself on Ivy but she fought back — '

'You're loco! I wanted to help get the

sonuvers who killed Randy, but you'd already gone. So I stayed to help Ivy get your place ready to prove-up. Hell's teeth! I'd never harm her! Never!' Wylie was breathing hard now, eyes wide, moving agitatedly.

'Maybe it started out as a joke — got out of hand,' Benbow continued, his own voice with a slight tremble in it now. His eyes were narrowed and steady on Wylie. 'Bad enough for Ivy to reach for her derringer and give you both shots — It's only a .32 — she never wanted to kill anyone with it. The slugs slowed you down but by then you'd've been ragin', out of your head. Had to keep her quiet so she never told anyone. 'Specially me. But I guess she fought you, and . . . That about how it happened, Wylie?'

Wylie glared, nostrils flaring, not answering.

'When you realized what you'd done, you panicked — knew there'd be no escape from this. Unless you could put the blame on someone else. Why not

Ryan's bunch? They'd been here, had a score to settle with both of us. You were wounded and could act it up, you could even be a hero, pulling poor Ivy from the fire.'

An unearthly howl escaped Wylie. His face crumbled.

'Aw, Christ, Chance, I never meant for it to happen. I was in love with her! Scoff if you like but as soon as I laid eyes on her I-I wanted her. But I knew she was yours and . . . ' He drew down a deep breath, made a helpless gesture with his left hand. And while the brief movement momentarily distracted Benbow, Wylie drew his six-gun, firing instantly.

Benbow was knocked off his feet, but he started to twist before he hit the ground. He had enough impetus to shoulder-roll and came up to his knees, Colt hammering.

Wylie staggered, fought to keep balance, trying to bring his gun around. Benbow shot him again and he dropped to his knees, sobbing, blood filling his mouth, staining his chest. He tumbled forward, slid down to within a few feet of Benbow.

His glazing eyes sought the man who had shot him. He spat blood and, as his head fell back, gasped,

'S-sorry — Chance — sorry . . . I . . . '

'Go to hell, Wylie.'

But Wylie was past hearing anything.

Benbow sat back with a thump and looked down at his bleeding side. It was mighty painful and he knew it would hurt a lot more before it got better. He could make it down as far as Cartwright's, then there would likely be a long spell in Doc Sharpe's infirmary . . .

But that would be OK.

He had a lot to think about.

THE END

We do hope that you have enjoyed reading this large print book.

Did you know that all of our titles are available for purchase?

We publish a wide range of high quality large print books including:
**Romances, Mysteries, Classics
General Fiction
Non Fiction and Westerns**

Special interest titles available in large print are:
**The Little Oxford Dictionary
Music Book, Song Book
Hymn Book, Service Book**

Also available from us courtesy of Oxford University Press:
**Young Readers' Dictionary
(large print edition)
Young Readers' Thesaurus
(large print edition)**

For further information or a free brochure, please contact us at:
**Ulverscroft Large Print Books Ltd.,
The Green, Bradgate Road, Anstey,
Leicester, LE7 7FU, England.
Tel:** (00 44) **0116 236 4325
Fax:** (00 44) **0116 234 0205**

Other titles in the
Linford Western Library:

LAST MILE TO NOGALES

Ryan Bodie

Nogales was a hell town, in the heart of the desert. Its single claim to fame was its band of deadly guns-for-hire who lived there, especially Ryan Coder, whom some saw as the gun king. Yet Coder found his life on the line when he hired out to the king of Chad Valley and was pitted against Holly, the youngest and deadliest gunslinger of them all. Would Coder end up just another notch on Holly's gun?

THE DEVIL'S RIDER

Lance Howard

When vicious outlaw Jeremy Trask escapes the hangman's noose, he rides into Baton Ridge on a mission of revenge and bloodlust. It had been a year since he'd murdered manhunter Jim Darrow's brother in cold blood. Now, along with the sole survivor of the massacre, a young homeless widow named Spring Treller, Darrow vows to hunt down the outlaw — this time to finish him for good. But will he survive the deadly reception the outlaw has waiting?